Stonewall Pride

WeHo 2019 Stonewall Pride (50th Anniversary Edition)

Sherryl D. Hancock

Copyright © Sherryl D. Hancock 2020

All rights reserved. No part of this publication may be reproduced, stored in or introduced into a retrieval system or transmitted in any form or by any means, electronic, mechanical, photocopying, recording or otherwise without prior written permission from the publisher.

This is a work of fiction. Names, characters, places and incidents are either the product of the author's imagination or are used fictitiously, and any resemblance to any person or persons, living or dead, events or locales is entirely coincidental.

Published by Vulpine Press in the United Kingdom in 2020

ISBN: 978-1-83919-052-0

Cover by Claire Wood
Cover photo credit: Tirzah D. Hancock

www.vulpine-press.com

For everyone in the LGBTQI community that not only began the war, but who fight it to this very day. You made this and books like it possible. You made it legal for me to marry my soul mate and best friend. You made it safer for us to walk the streets holding hands. You made life better. I promise to keep up the fight through my writing. Thank you for all you did and continue to do!

Acknowledgments

Thank you to Sarah Markel, another amazing lesfic writer, who told me her Pride story, and inspired a section of this book. Thank you, Sarah!

Also to my publisher, Vulpine Press, who never shrinks from letting me tell my stories! Thank you to Rob Johnson, Sarah Hembrow, Toby Selwyn, Kia Thomas, and everyone at Vulpine for helping me do my small part in the movement. I appreciate you!

Also in the WeHo series:

When Love Wins
When Angels Fall
Break in the Storm
Turning Tables
Marking Time
Jet Blue
Water Under the Bridge
Vendetta
Gray Skies
Everything to Everyone
Lightning Strykes
In Plain Sight
Quid Pro Qup
For the Telling
Between Heaven and Hell
Taking Chances
Darkness Past

Chapter 1

"Wind that one way up," Memphis told the artist standing in the sound booth, twirling her finger in the air to indicate what she was asking for.

"Again?" the woman complained.

"You want it to sound good, right?" It wasn't really a question.

The woman sighed loudly. "Fine!" she yelled back.

Memphis chuckled to herself; this one wasn't even famous yet and she already had an attitude.

As they continued to work, Memphis thought about her upcoming trip to San Diego. She was excited about getting to DJ again. She hadn't been doing much spinning since she'd started working for BJ Sparks as a sound tech, and for directors like Legend Azaria, helping with movie scores. It was an awesome life, but she did miss the fun of the clubs, and feeling the crowd responding to the music she played. She imagined it was a high not unlike what performers felt when they sang for cheering crowds. It was her tiny bit of fame. Fame… it was a word that still scared her—the idea of people knowing her name, recognizing her. She'd spent so much of her life hiding who she really was, since escaping a cult that would have married her to a man at sixteen, who already had many other wives. People knowing her scared her. She'd been through a lot in her past, but she was doing her best to stay in the present. Accepting the offer to DJ at a very popular San Diego LGBTQ club called Gossip Grill was a step in that direction. That didn't mean she wasn't nervous about it though.

"What's on?" came an Irish accent from behind her later that afternoon.

Memphis turned to see Quinn standing in the doorway to the studio and she smiled widely at her friend.

"What are you doing here?" Memphis asked, even as she jumped up to hug the other woman.

"Meetin' with Beege," Quinn told her, glancing behind Memphis at the girl singing in the sound booth. "Who's that?"

Memphis glanced over her shoulder at the girl, shaking her head. "An up-and-coming pain in the ass."

"Lovely." Quinn rolled her eyes. "You got some time for lunch?"

"Sounds great!" Memphis enthused, glancing at her watch. "Gimme a minute."

A few minutes later they walked out to the parking lot of Badlands Records.

"Aw you brought the new toy…" Memphis grinned widely.

"She needs my time," Quinn told Memphis with a bright smile.

"She's so pretty," Memphis said, sliding a hand appreciatively over the rear fender of Quinn's latest acquisition.

Xandy had bought Quinn the $229,000 1968 Ford Mustang Shelby for her birthday. Everyone at the party had been completely bowled over, but Xandy knew Quinn's thing for classic muscle cars and knew that it would make her girlfriend happy. Quinn had been completely floored by the gift, and still couldn't believe Xandy had been so generous.

As the engine started with a raucous growl, a euphoric smile lit up the Irishwoman's face.

"Nice!" Memphis enthused, knowing that Quinn loved the car.

"She is, ain't she?"

"Oh yeah." Memphis nodded excitedly.

They roared out of the parking lot and down the strip heading for their favorite hole-in-the-wall Mexican restaurant.

"So what were you meeting with BJ about?" Memphis queried.

Quinn made a disgusted noise in the back of her throat as she rolled her eyes. "He wants me to protect Billy."

"Montague?" Memphis named her old nemesis. Billy Montague, the highly talented lead singer of Billy and the Kid, was a prima donna to the nth power, and a pain in the ass to pretty much everyone who dealt with her.

"The very one," Quinn replied.

"What's her problem now?" Memphis asked.

"Apparently she opened that mouth of hers one too many times about DDog and now he's making threats…" Quinn's mouth curled in derision at the thought. DDog was a rapper who'd been reputed to be part of a violent gang before getting into music. He'd been known for flashing gang symbols and guns in photos and videos. He was no one to be messed with.

"Might serve Billy right."

"Yeah, but shootin' yer mouth off shouldn't get your husband and your kid threatened."

"Skyler can take care of himself," Memphis pointed out. Skyler Kristiani was a former narcotics officer who still had a concealed weapons permit to protect his rock star wife.

"He doesn't have eyes in the back of his head, DDog is hardcore."

"True," Memphis agreed. "So you gonna do it?"

"Mackie wants me to," Quinn said, talking about her boss, John Machiavelli, the co-owner of Mach 3, a private security team.

"You hate protecting entertainment people."

"Yeah, that's why he's gonna pay me an obscene amount of money to do it," Quinn quipped.

Memphis laughed, nodding. She respected Quinn Kavanaugh; the woman was one serious bad ass. If anyone could protect Billy Montague and her big mouth, it was Quinn.

"So, I got some news," Memphis said.

"What's up?"

"I've been asked to do some DJing down in San Diego next month."

Quinn looked surprised, but then she nodded, glancing over at her young friend. "Where at?"

"A bar called Gossip Grill. It's a girl bar in Hillcrest."

"Gay part o' town?" Quinn asked, her accent clipped.

Memphis grinned. "Do I DJ anywhere else?"

"You don't DJ anywhere these days," Quinn replied snidely. "Now that you're so sought after and all…"

"Quit it." Memphis laughed. "I've missed DJing."

Quinn's look sobered as she nodded. "I know ya have. So this'll be good."

"Yeah, the owner was saying that she could probably get me a gig with the Pride festival too."

"Probably?" Quinn scoffed. "They'd wet themselves to get you to DJ for 'em."

Memphis pressed her lips together, always enjoying her friend's praise. She never felt like a big shot, but her close friends always reminded her that she was indeed a big deal in the music community. Quinn was one of her best friends, someone she felt safe with. Quinn had come to her defense so often, when it counted the most, and it meant the world to Memphis.

"So when's this?" Quinn asked, glancing over at Memphis.

"Mid-July."

Quinn nodded, narrowing her eyes slightly. She knew that Memphis got really nervous around crowds of strangers. She also knew that Memphis wouldn't ask for her protection, but she felt the need to protect the younger girl anyway. Quinn and Remington LaRoché had grown close to her during a concert tour a few years before. When Memphis had gone off to confront the cult that had been stalking her, Quinn and Remington had led the charge to get her back. Memphis had been severely hurt during that time; the cult members had tried to cut the gay out of her, trying to carve away all the Pride tattoos she had. It had been a terrifying incident and had stayed with Memphis. For all she tried to pretend it didn't, Quinn knew it was never far from the girl's mind.

"So, what's say I come down with ya?" Quinn asked as she pulled into the restaurant parking lot.

Memphis glanced over at her friend. "But what about Billy?"

"I'll get Mackie ta babysit for a little bit," Quinn drawled.

Memphis bit her lip, her desire not to be a drain on her friends warring with her desire to feel safe. "You sure? I talked to Sky, she's gonna talk to Jet about going down."

Quinn nodded, glad to hear their other friends had the same idea; everyone loved the sweet spirit that was Memphis, loved it and wanted to protect it.

"I could take my girl here on her first road trip," Quinn said, grinning. "Xandy and Wynter are still gonna be out on tour at that point, so I'm betting I could con Remi into comin' along too."

"That'd be cool," Memphis said, secretly happy that Quinn really seemed to want to come.

"Well, I'll talk to Remi then." Quinn winked. "We'll make it a trip to remember."

***

"Memphis is really going to do it?" Remington asked as Quinn nodded.

"I think she misses the spin." Quinn smirked, sipping her beer as they sat on the patio of Wynter and Remi's house.

"She's been too cooped up lately," Remington agreed.

"So you in then?" Quinn asked.

Remington nodded. "I think it could be fun."

"I'm thinking of asking the young'uns to go with us."

Remington considered for a moment. "I suppose that would be more fun for Memphis than us old hats."

"Eh, speak for yerself, mate!" Quinn laughed, then grew serious. "I just figure more eyes, ya know?"

Remington winced. The specter of "the family," the cult Memphis had escaped from, still loomed around the group. Their leader had been killed in prison, but that hadn't disbanded the group, and it was a source of constant caution for Remington and Quinn. They desperately wanted to shield Memphis from any more emotional or physical damage.

***

"How'd you like to hit Pride in San Diego this year?" Skyler asked Jet without preamble as soon as Jet answered her phone.

"And good morning…" Jet said, grinning as she fixed her coffee, what her wife, Fadiyah, called her "Jet fuel" due to its strength and its use for calming Jet's ADHD.

"Yadda, yadda," Skyler intoned.

"When is it?" Jet asked.

"Starts July 12," Skyler answered, leaning back in her chair, one foot on the chair across from her, cigarette in hand.

"And Memphis is DJing?" Jet set down her coffee, glancing over at Fadiyah who'd just entered the room.

"Yeah, at Gossip Grill. You know how Memphis gets in strange surroundings, figured she could use the support. Think you can break away?"

Jet leaned over to kiss her wife's lips, even as she glanced at the calendar on the fridge. "Shit, Fadi's got testing that week."

"Think she'd let you come down alone? You know, without your ADHD ass there pestering her so she can actually study?" Skyler asked with a grin.

"Bite me, Sky," Jet responded automatically, but still chuckling, knowing her friend was likely right about that. It drove her crazy when Fadiyah had to study—it meant they couldn't go out, couldn't do anything because Fadiyah was serious about finishing her nursing degree this year.

"You haven't had your shots," Skyler replied, laughing as she threw another ball for Benny, her husky, and watched him bound after it excitedly.

Jet didn't bother to reply, eyeing Fadiyah as she bustled about the kitchen making her morning tea. "I'll talk to Fadi and let you know. Would you want to take the bikes? Make it a Lost Bois outing?"

The Lost Bois was a group she and Skyler had started with some of their younger friends who also rode motorcycles. They would get together with Memphis, Harley, Talon, Dakota, and Cody and take rides to different locations.

"Oh, good idea, that'll make it easier to park."

"Right, that's all I was thinkin'…" Jet said with an evil laugh.

"You never change," Skyler said, amazed that her friend still thoroughly enjoyed making the women drool. A hot butch on a bike was always a draw. "We should check with the rest of the bois to see if they want to go."

"Talon's out of town with Legend and the crew, but everyone else would be good to go, maybe. We could even ride with Dykes on Bikes, if we let them know soon enough," Jet commented, mentioning the time-honored tradition of the group who led the beginning of the parade in various rainbow and leather regalia riding motorcycles.

"We could," Skyler replied. That was about the only way Devin was likely to agree to her riding her motorcycle down to San Diego.

"You could get Devin to follow us in the Hummer."

"Yeah, she'll love that." Skyler rolled her eyes, knowing her wife would probably hate driving behind them. She was right, as she found out a few minutes after she'd hung up with Jet.

"You know I hate watching you ride—it freaks me out every time someone gets too close to you!"

"Well, I know you don't like to ride bitch…" Skyler commented blithely.

"Uh, no," Devin agreed, then sighed in defeat. "Fine, I'll drive behind, but you're gonna have to get someone to ride with me."

"Well, I doubt Kieran will want to ride on the bike with Memphis, so I'm sure she'd be happy to ride with ya. Cody and Dakota will probably go, so maybe Jaz and Kenna too."

"Yeah, that might be fun." Devin smiled, thinking that the girls would be great fun to travel down to San Diego with. "Where are we going to stay?"

"Dunno, I'll get some ideas from Cat. She's from San Diego, she'll know."

"Is Cat going?"

"Dunno… I guess we'll find out."

***

"Harley, have you heard a word I've said?" Shiloh queried.

"I, uh… what?" Harley replied, her mind in a hundred different places at once as she drove in morning traffic.

Shiloh laughed softly, shaking her head. Harley tended to be more distracted when she couldn't drive at top speed. As her long-time assistant, and girlfriend, Shiloh knew Harley's habits so was rarely offended when her ADHD partner wasn't paying attention to her.

"That's a no." Shiloh pursed her lips, reaching out her hand to cover Harley's on the gear shift, physically trying to draw Harley's attention to her. "Can you focus on me for a minute please?"

Harley grimaced as she nodded. "Sorry, babe."

"It's okay, I just need you to hear some of this, so we don't have issues today."

"Got it, no issues," Harley stated succinctly.

"Okay, so you have three meetings today, one of which is with Midnight and I'm gonna need you to pay attention to your reminders so you're not late for that one, okay?"

"Yes, ma'am," Harley replied, feeling her iWatch on her wrist vibrate. She glanced at it and saw the green word bubble for a text message and stared at it for a long moment.

Shiloh narrowed her eyes. "I thought I activated the 'do not disturb' on that…" Her tone indicated her suspicion even as she said it.

"Uh…" Harley stammered guiltily.

"Harley Marie Davidson!" Shiloh exclaimed, laughing as the guilt-ridden look crossed Harley's face. "You know you're not supposed to be texting and driving, and you know you can't resist text messages…"

"I know, I know…" Harley agreed. "I think when I did that latest update it dropped the block and I just didn't fix it."

"'Cause you love getting text messages…"

"Well…" Harley rolled her eyes.

"Give me your phone, I'll tell you what it says…" Shiloh offered.

Harley dutifully handed her phone to Shiloh.

Shiloh punched in the password, still amused by her girlfriend's chagrin. Harley was forever trying to keep her ADHD mind occupied. Shiloh was forever worried about what could happen if Harley's need to read text messages and her need to drive at breakneck speeds collided. Harley drove a Stillen Supercharger 370Z sports car, and she rarely drove slowly, unless traffic made it necessary. Because of her ADHD, things easily distracted her. A lot of the time it was work, and she was often hyper-focused to the point of forgetting meetings. The iWatch had been a blessing and a curse—it helped to track Harley down when she'd wandered off in search of caffeine or a snack during the day, but it also allowed her to read text messages when she shouldn't. The 'do not disturb' feature was handy, in that it would keep Harley from getting messages when Shiloh didn't want her to, like when she was already in a meeting or in the car. It didn't, however, help if the feature dropped upon a reset.

"Okay, so it's a message from Sky. She says that a group of them are going to San Diego for Pride and did you want to go?"

"Why San Diego?" Harley asked, zipping between two cars as traffic momentarily let up.

Shiloh tapped out the message and sent it back to Skyler. She flicked Harley's ear a few moments later when she started to look at her watch for the response when it came in. Harley simply laughed in response.

"She said that Memphis is spinning at Gossip Grill down there for Pride," Shiloh told her. "Don't make me take that watch off of you while you're driving…"

"When is Pride? This month?"

"LA Pride is this month," Shiloh said, looking for San Diego's information. "San Diego Pride is July 12 this year."

Harley thought about it and ran through her list of projects in her head, trying to determine if she'd have time. Her fingers tapped on the steering wheel, her nearly constant energy escaping in the smallest ways.

Shiloh watched Harley's face as her mind raced. She knew that Harley needed the break, she'd be exhausted in another month or so.

"This might be a good time for that break we've been talking about, babe," Shiloh put in hopefully.

Harley screwed up her face as she hated the idea of a "break," but she also knew she needed one at some point. It was that or her body would force her into a break by getting sick.

Finally, she relented. "Okay, run it by Rayden to make sure she's cool with it."

"Rayden's been telling me to schedule you a break," Shiloh informed her with a wink. "I'll let her know we've decided."

"Always ahead of me somehow…" Harley muttered, not unhappily. She loved that Shiloh cared enough about her to take care of her.

There'd been so many women in her life that hadn't bothered to understand her way of doing things. Harley knew that she was a handful for most people, and that Shiloh was a very special person to be willing to work with her and be her lover and friend too. For her part, Harley tried to be worthy of such love and devotion; when she focused her attention on Shiloh, it was with a great deal of tenderness and generosity. Their relationship worked because they understood each other, but Shiloh was also the type of woman to tell Harley when something was wrong, and was willing to try and work through things. It made all the difference. Too many women before hadn't been willing to tell Harley what she was doing that was frustrating to them—they expected her to know. Shiloh wasn't like that and Harley loved her all the more for it.

***

McKenna Falco smiled softly when she opened the bedroom door to note that her wife lay snuggled under the covers. Cody had been gone for over a week and McKenna had missed her as she always did. As an undercover agent for a task force that did its best to track down and stop human traffickers, Cody had to disappear sometimes. It wasn't something that McKenna liked, and it was definitely something she worried about constantly when her wife was gone. But it was always a wonderful sight to behold when Cody was suddenly, unexpectedly, home.

McKenna moved about the room quietly, going in to take a quick shower before she slid into bed with her wife. Cody stirred immediately, glancing at the clock on the nightstand.

"Were you on tonight?" Cody asked.

McKenna nodded, knowing that Cody was referring to working at the shelter. McKenna worked at the LGBT teen shelter that Savannah, Cody's mother, ran. Savannah and McKenna took turns staying late to ensure that their kids were "tucked in" for the night.

Cody leaned in, kissing her wife.

"Cody, you look so tired…" McKenna whispered, reaching up to touch Cody's forehead.

"Rough week." Cody's voice backed up that statement, but McKenna sensed something else in Cody's look.

"How rough?"

Cody's lips twitched as she reached up to rub her eyebrow with her finger, a sure sign that she was trying to avoid something. She moved to sit up, rubbing her face. McKenna sat up too, knowing she was not going to like what was about to be said.

"Cody, how rough?" McKenna repeated.

Cody chewed at the inside of her cheek, debating telling McKenna, but knowing she would expect McKenna to be honest with her.

"I missed my pills a couple of times," Cody said, referring to the lithium she took for bipolar depression.

"Oh babe…" McKenna grimaced. It would have made things so much harder for Cody in an undercover situation.

"I know, I know." Cody nodded, biting her bottom lip as she winced. "Moms would kill me. Things just go a bit hairy and I couldn't take the time, you know?" The question was a plea.

"I know," McKenna said, nodding, knowing that Lyric and Savannah, Cody's mothers, would indeed be furious with their daughter for missing her meds. McKenna was doing her best to control her upset, reminding Cody of the consequences of her not taking her medication.

They were both quiet for a minute. McKenna reached up, taking Cody's head in her hands and pulled it down to hers, hugging her wife as she debated saying what was in her mind.

"Maybe you shouldn't continue with undercover work…" McKenna broached the subject gently.

Cody's head snapped up immediately. "No," was the vehement answer.

"Cody…"

"No, Kenna, no!" Cody exclaimed. "I'm not quitting doing this. It's too damned important."

McKenna forced herself to remain calm. Projecting her fears onto Cody wouldn't help the situation at all. Cody had a PhD in psychology, like McKenna did, and she'd know immediately that McKenna was using it on her, so it wasn't the way to go.

"There is a lot you can do without going undercover, Cody," McKenna said softly. "You could work with informants, develop new relationships that don't entail you pretending to be something you're not anymore…"

Cody's sharp look had McKenna's voice trailing off. "You think I didn't take my pills on purpose."

"No," McKenna said, shaking her head, "I think that putting yourself in a vulnerable position, like you were when you were young, takes you too far down, and your own mental health takes a back seat."

Cody looked back at her for a long moment. It was obvious she wanted to disagree with her wife, but it was clear that something McKenna had said rang true. Cody pressed her lips together, sighing as she nodded her head.

"You might be right about that."

McKenna nodded sympathetically. Cody battled constantly with her depression. Fortunately, her degree in psychology helped her understand what was happening in her own head. It was something that they had a common bond over; McKenna understood her wife's depression and could see things more clearly than Cody could, and she also knew the best way to get her wife to see things. They were a good match. They had been from the first time they'd met. Even if McKenna had been married to a man at the time, and had thought Cody was an underage girl in the group home.

"So, I heard that some of the group are headed to San Diego next month," Cody said, wanting to change the subject. McKenna knew it didn't mean that Cody wouldn't think about what was said, it just meant she needed time to process.

"Yeah? What for?"

"Pride, Memphis is spinning."

"Wow, she hasn't done that in a long time. So are you thinking we should go?"

Cody grinned. "Yeah, I think I'd like to… Jet and Sky are going to ride their bikes. I was thinking of asking Mom if I could borrow the Leggera."

McKenna looked shocked. "You think Lyric will let you borrow that?"

Lyric's motorcycle was a Ducati Superleggera, a sixty-five-thousand-dollar motorcycle and her prized possession.

"I'm hoping…" Cody said, grinning, her gold eyes sparkling in the semi-darkness of the room.

"Oh lord." McKenna rolled her eyes, wondering how that was going to go.

***

"I don't know, Code," Lyric said, "that's a lot of bike for you…"

"You're saying I can't handle it?" Cody replied, looking offended.

"I'm saying it's a lot of bike," Lyric replied, knowing her daughter's penchant for speeding. "And how will McKenna get to San Diego?"

"Not on the back of a motorcycle, I can assure you," McKenna answered with a patient smile.

Savannah chuckled as she sipped her coffee.

"You stay out of this," Cody told her other mother good-naturedly, then she looked back at Lyric. "Devin is driving down in her Hummer, Kenna will ride with her."

"And you're okay with that?" Lyric asked her daughter-in-law.

"I'm fine with it," McKenna assured her.

Lyric's lips twitched. McKenna could tell that her mother-in-law had hoped to get an argument from Cody's wife, and therefore make it so she wouldn't have to decide on whether or not to loan her beloved Leggera to her sometimes irresponsible, speed-demon of a daughter. Glancing over at Savannah, Lyric wanted to see what her wife thought. Their eyes met and, as if by telepathy, Lyric nodded, knowing that Savannah was saying to give Cody a chance to prove she could handle the privilege of riding such an expensive bike.

Sighing, Lyric said, "Okay, Code… but you make sure you're super careful with her. You got me?"

"Promise!" Cody said, jumping up to hug her mother as Savannah and McKenna looked on fondly.

Chapter 2

"You need me to train you to what?" Kai Temple asked, not sure she'd heard correctly.

"To be a smoke jumper," the other woman explained, her hazel eyes sparkling with subdued excitement. The idea of training with the now famous Kai Temple was beyond her comprehension. As it was, she couldn't believe she'd been lucky enough to land a meeting with the trainer.

"What does a smoke jumper do?" Kai asked, grinning crookedly.

White teeth flashed in a wide smile. "Jumps out of perfectly good airplanes to go and fight wildfires."

"Wow," Kai said, looking fairly impressed with the notion. "Can you elaborate exactly what you need?"

"I need to be able to hump one hundred and ten pounds of gear three miles in ninety minutes, over rough terrain."

Kai stared back at the young woman sitting in front of her, she looked like she might weigh a hundred pounds and definitely didn't look strong enough to lift fifty pounds let alone one hundred and ten.

"You want to do this why?"

"Because some man told me I couldn't," was the immediate response, said with enough barely subdued ire that Kai liked her instantly.

Women were told too often they couldn't handle jobs men could do, but more so in the world of military, law enforcement, and firefighting. Kai was all so happy to help prove those men wrong.

"Well, I'm willing to train you, but the work is going to be on you. If you don't commit fully, then you won't get the result you're looking for."

"I want this, I promise you that, and I'll give you everything I have to get it."

"That's exactly what I need to hear," Kai told her. "We'll start tomorrow, Ms. Salire."

"Phoenix," the woman replied.

Kai smiled, inclining her head. "Be here tomorrow, 7 a.m."

"I'll be here," Phoenix replied, smiling brightly.

"Yeah, we'll see if you're still smiling tomorrow."

***

"She's from where?" Remington asked, lifting a beer to her lips.

"San Diego," Kai answered leaning back in her chair and glancing back at her wife who was heading toward their table with their drinks. They were gathered at The Club, their usual hangout on Friday nights.

"And she wants to do what?" Cody asked, still trying to catch up to the conversation.

"To be a smoke jumper." Kai replied.

"Which is…?" Dakota asked.

"Apparently people who parachute into remote wildfires," Kai answered, sounding still awed by the very idea.

"That sounds a bit crazy…" Cody said, shaking her head.

"You mean, like running someone off a second story building to save your girl?" Dakota queried with a raised eyebrow.

"Shaddup," Cody muttered out of the side of her mouth as the others laughed.

A few years back, Cody had attacked a gang member who was holding her then girlfriend McKenna in a motel room on the second floor. When all else had failed, Cody had rushed the man, charging forward to the point of running him out of the room and off the second-floor balcony. It had been a testament to her love for McKenna but had also scared the life out of her mothers. Fortunately, Cody had survived with minor injuries; the gang member had not. Enough time had passed that her friends were able to joke about it now.

"Now that's crazy," McKenna put in, her eyes sparkling with humor.

"So says the psychologist," Dakota said, winking at McKenna.

"Seriously?" Cody queried, giving her wife a narrowed look.

McKenna merely chuckled, giving her wife's hand a squeeze as she took a sip of her wine.

"So why's she training with you?" Cody asked, hurrying on when Kai made an offended grunt. "I just mean, why does she need to?"

Dakota laughed gleefully at Cody's embarrassment at her blunder. Kai Temple was well known for being a trainer to the stars; she'd trained Remington LaRoché, an MMA champion, for many of her fights and had gotten superstar Riley Taylor ready for a starring role in an academy award-winning performance. It was an industry-wide fact that if a person needed to get physically ready to take on a difficult role or task, Kai Temple was who you wanted to work with.

"Well, it sounds like it's not an easy job to get, and she wants to kill it," Kai told her, supreme confidence in her voice.

"And she just happened to look you up?" Dakota asked, curious now too.

"I guess she heard about me somehow through Gage and Gunn."

"Well, that makes sense," Dakota added. "Firefighting and all."

"I guess it's more the piloting thing," Kai told them. "Her dad runs a flight school out of San Diego—met Gage and Gunn that way."

"Aw." Dakota nodded. "Or that."

"Or that," Cody echoed snidely.

"Shaddup," Dakota growled, grinning as she did.

"So," Kai began, shifting to look at Dakota, "when am I getting that second set of showers?" Kai rented her training studio space from Dakota and her wife, Jazmine.

"I need to come look at the space tomorrow to take some measurements, say about ten?" Dakota asked.

"That should work, I'll be there with Phoenix."

"The new kid?" Cody asked.

"Yes," Kai answered.

"Her name is Phoenix?" Dakota asked.

"Yep," Kai replied. "Salire."

Cody chuckled. "Her name is Phoenix Salire?"

"Yes, why?" Kai was bewildered by Cody's amusement.

"Is she Italian?"

"Got me," Kai said.

"I'm betting she is," Cody said, still smirking. "Salire means 'rise' in Italian."

"So basically Phoenix Rising?" Dakota said.

"Basically," Cody answered.

"Enteresan…" Remington muttered in Creole, saying "interesting."

"Definitely," Kai murmured.

***

Cody was just finishing getting dressed when her wife's distressed scream had her running to the front door.

"What! What is it?" Cody asked, her eyes scanning the front drive where McKenna was pointing excitedly, practically bouncing on the balls of her feet in her excitement.

"There, look, behind my car! I thought it was a kitten!"

"What the…" Cody said as she walked cautiously toward the odd-looking creature. It was small, with greyish-brown short hair and a long tail.

"Is it a rat?" McKenna asked, stepping toward Cody cautiously.

"No, it doesn't look like one," Cody said, noting that the little creature wasn't moving. "It is even alive?" she asked more to herself than to her wife.

"I don't know, I saw it in my backup camera. I thought it was a kitten so I slammed on the breaks, but then when I got out… It looked weird… I didn't know what else to do."

"But scream for the other city dweller that knows jack shit about wildlife…" Cody muttered amusedly.

"Oh stop… Look! It's moving!"

"Kenna grab me a box and a blanket, I'll see if there's a wildlife rescue that can take it."

An hour later, Cody walked into Kai's studio with a small box in hand.

Kai looked up from where she stood at the weight bench, spotting for Phoenix. "Morning, Code, what's that?" she asked, indicating the box.

"I dunno, some little creature Kenna almost took out with her car this morning," Cody said, setting the box down. "I'm trying to take it to wildlife rescue, but they're not open for another hour…" Her voice trailed off as she looked curiously at the woman training with Kai, then her gaze shifted to Kai expectantly.

"Oh, yeah, Phoenix, this is Cody Falco, Cody, this is Phoenix Salire."

"Hi," Cody said. She stepped over to the weight bench and extended her hand as Phoenix sat up and took it, her hazel eyes looking into the box still in Cody's other hand.

"That's an opossum," Phoenix said.

"It is?" Cody queried.

"Yeah," Phoenix said, reaching over to take the box, and gently lifting the small creature out. "Looks about maybe a month old… maybe forty days. Wildlife probably won't take it."

"How do you know?" Cody asked curiously.

"I spent summers in Redding with my grandfather. He's a vet, saw a lot of them."

"So why won't wildlife rescue take it?"

"Because they're really tough to save at this age. Their mouths are sealed shut at this point, gonna take a lot of work to feed it."

"So I should just let it die?" Cody asked, looking sick at the idea.

Phoenix shrugged. "I can take it for you."

"To let it die?" Cody repeated.

Phoenix chuckled, shaking her head. "No, I mean I'll take care of it."

"Take care of it how?" Cody asked, looking suspicious.

"As in do my best to save it," Phoenix replied, unaffected by Cody's suspicious look.

"You know what to do?" Kai asked, surprised by this information.

Again Phoenix shrugged. "Like I said, Granddad is a vet. I've worked with all kinds of animals. I'll need to find a craft store that's open, and a store to buy some things."

"I can take you to get some stuff," Cody said, suddenly wanting to help save the animal.

"That would help—I don't know where anything is here," Phoenix said, reaching for her sweatshirt hanging on the weight bench. She glanced at Kai. "Can we reschedule for tomorrow?"

"No way, you come back here when you get what you need, this I gotta see," Kai said, grinning.

"Whoa…" Phoenix said when she saw Cody's car. Her hand slid along the side of the vehicle reverently. "What is this?"

Cody smiled proudly. "She's a 66 Ferrari 275 GTB."

"A whatta whatta?" Phoenix replied, shaking her head. "Never mind, this is one seriously hot car…"

Cody laughed, nodding her head. "Yeah, yeah she is."

A few moments later, Cody appreciated the look of complete rapture on Phoenix's face as she started the car up with a throaty growl of the engine.

"Heaven…" Phoenix murmured.

"Every damn day." Cody smiled widely.

As they drove down the road, Phoenix glanced over at the other woman. She figured Cody was about her age; with the spiked blond hair and easy grin, she had to be young. She wondered what the other woman did for a living that she could afford a car like this one.

"So what do you do?" Phoenix asked without preamble.

"I'm a cop," Cody replied simply.

"Cops make a lot of money in LA?"

Cody chuckled. "Not really, no."

"Ferraris cheaper than I think then?"

Cody laughed outright at that question. "No, but my mom helped me build her. Ferraris are kind of a family thing for us Falcos."

"I see," Phoenix replied, sounding like she truly didn't.

Cody glanced over as she drove, taking in the longish hair on top, with the shaved lower section. She wasn't sure how old Phoenix was, but she sensed something about the girl that read kindred spirit to Cody.

"Thanks for being willing to take care of the little guy," Cody said, her eyes softening. "My wife will be happy to hear he's in good hands."

"Wife?" Phoenix repeated, raising an eyebrow. "You're married?"

"Yeah," Cody said, smiling fondly. "McKenna kind of has this thing for saving orphans. So…"

"Orphans?"

"Of all species," Cody added.

"Including you?"

"Including me," Cody affirmed.

"But you said your mom…" Phoenix pointed out.

"My adopted mom, well, moms really."

"Moms," Phoenix repeated. "Your parents are lesbians?"

"Best kind," Cody enthused.

"Probably better than mine," Phoenix said, her look sour.

Cody's senses became on high alert. "That bad?" she asked casually.

Phoenix shrugged. "Could have been worse, I guess."

Cody narrowed her eyes slightly. "Well, you're still here, that's what counts, right?"

"Damned skippy," Phoenix replied.

Cody was silent, but she knew she was right about this one: Phoenix was someone like her, she felt it and she was usually right about this kind of thing. She further sensed it as they made their way through the craft store, when the woman they asked about syringes gave them both an odd look. Phoenix's chin went up, as her eyes narrowed and her lips tightened. Later in the grocery store a man bumped into Phoenix, and Cody noted the way the younger woman stood her ground, looking up at the man warily, even as the man simply moved on as if he hadn't even noticed her.

"So what are we looking for?" Cody asked to distract Phoenix.

"Eggs, evaporated milk, liquid pet vitamins if they have any," Phoenix replied, moving forward, but glancing over her shoulder circumspectly. "We need a heating pad too. Gotta keep him warm."

They made their way through the store without any other incidents, but it was obvious to Cody that this girl was on her guard all the time. She didn't seem to trust many people; her eyes watched everyone around her constantly, as if expecting an attack.

On the drive back to Kai's, Cody broached the topic as gently as could. "So, I'm guessing you've been around a bit, huh?"

"Around?" Phoenix queried warily.

"You know, around bad shit," Cody said, keeping her tone casual.

Phoenix's lips twitched. "I've dealt with issues in my lifetime, yeah… why?"

Cody shrugged. "I guess I recognize the signs."

Phoenix settled herself against the passenger door, turning to reassess Cody. It wasn't clear what she was looking for.

"The signs of what?"

"People like me," Cody said simply.

"Like you, how?"

"Just people who've been through things and have toughed it out."

"What did you tough out?" Phoenix asked, her tone skeptical.

Cody glanced over at the other woman sharply, her eyes flaring in immediate reaction to the tone. "More than you think, trust me."

Phoenix didn't reply, simply pursed her lips in circumspection. They were both silent for a few minutes and Cody made a point of calming herself. She hadn't appreciated Phoenix's tone. She knew that the other woman thought she was some spoiled rich kid because of the car and the two moms. But there was no way that Phoenix could know that Cody had been prostituted by a gang at the age of fifteen and had nearly lost her life a few years before, fighting back against that same gang.

"What kind of cop are you?" Phoenix asked a little while later, her tone of voice cautious.

"I work for a task force, we stop the trafficking of young women by gangs," Cody replied evenly.

Phoenix blinked a couple of times, sensing something in Cody's tone of voice. Maybe she'd had it wrong about Cody Falco. "How'd you get into that kind of thing?"

"Personal experience," Cody replied simply. She heard Phoenix's sharp intake of breath and got a little bit of satisfaction out of it.

They pulled up in front of the gym at that point. Cody got out of the car without another word. Phoenix got out a minute later and followed Cody inside.

With a little effort, they'd got a bowl to mix formula for the opossum in, and Kai, Cody, and now Dakota, who'd arrived while they'd been gone, watched in fascination as Phoenix used the tiny syringe to feed the little creature. The syringe had a tiny tip but, even so, it took Phoenix a bit of effort to get it between the little animal's lips. When she finally managed the opossum ate greedily, making little squeaking sounds as it did.

"Holy shit, that's amazing!" Dakota exclaimed.

"Yeah, he's really young," Phoenix said, peering up at the newcomer with the short dark hair, "but he's eating pretty good. That's a good sign."

"So how often do you have to feed the little guy?" Kai asked.

"Every two hours or so."

"Jesus, like a baby," Cody said.

"That's what he is," Phoenix said, rubbing the opossum's little belly gently as she fed him. "Wonder how my hotel's gonna feel about my new roommate," she mused.

"You're staying in a hotel?" Dakota asked.

"Right now, till I can find something to rent short term."

"How long are you here for?" Cody asked, glancing at Dakota.

"Probably about four months," Phoenix replied.

"Anything?" Cody asked.

Phoenix glanced up, thinking Cody was asking her, but then saw she was looking at the newcomer.

"I probably have something," the dark-haired woman replied. "I'm Dakota by the way, and what Cody is asking is if I have a rental you can use."

"Oh, hey," Phoenix said, nodding.

"Dakota owns this studio with her girl, Jazmine. She also finds and fixes up houses, which she either sells off or rents out," Cody explained.

"I'm a contractor," Dakota said. "If you need a place, I can rent you something reasonable."

"That would be awesome," Phoenix said, feeling a bit overwhelmed by how nice these people were.

"Any friend of Cody's is a friend of mine," Dakota said, grinning.

Phoenix glanced up at Cody then, a look of chagrin on her face. "Are we?"

"Are we what?" Cody asked, tilting her head slightly.

"Friends?" Phoenix asked, looking vulnerable for the first time that morning.

Cody paused for a long moment, her look serious, but then a grin lightened her features. "Yeah, I think we can be." Phoenix looked instantly relieved. "You are keeping me out of hot water with the wife, after all," Cody continued, indicating the tiny creature looking sated in Phoenix's capable hands.

Phoenix laughed as she glanced down at the tiny life in her hands, surprised at how good it felt to be so easily accepted into an obviously tight-knit group. Things were looking up.

***

A couple of weeks later, the opossum, now named Bob because Phoenix named everything Bob, was doing well, and was on a regular feeding schedule of every three hours. Bob was a regular visitor to the gym, where Phoenix still trained with Kai.

One particular day, Kai had given Phoenix of series of tasks to do, and she was working out with a partner, Memphis Lassiter. The moment Kai sent the two off to the mats to do the circuit workout, Memphis made a beeline for the audio equipment in the room and hooked up her iPod. Music flowed through the speakers, but it was far from what Phoenix expected. The first song to come on was from the movie *Rocky IV* called 'Burning Heart.' It was obvious from Memphis' posture that the music put her at ease and they began their workout. As the music played on, Phoenix found herself perplexed by the mix of genres: the second song was by Linkin Park named 'A Light That Never Comes,' followed by a very obvious house music song that Phoenix didn't recognize, then a song by Lady Gaga named 'Telephone.'

"Uh…" Phoenix began as she and Memphis exchanged places on the two weight benches in their area, "Linkin Park and Gaga?"

Memphis laughed, looking far from offended, then she shrugged. "I'm a DJ, I love music, all kinds of music."

Phoenix blinked a couple of times, with a perplexed grin on her lips. "I'd say so…"

They continued to work out, and the next song that started made something click in Phoenix's mind. It was a mixture of songs that faded into each other in a very obviously manipulated way. Phoenix recognized it, but it took a few minutes for her to figure out where she knew it from.

"Holy shit, that's you!" she finally said, looking over at Memphis in obvious shock.

Memphis quirked her lips, grinning as she nodded. It was the entrance song that Memphis had mixed for Remington's last MMA fight with Akasha Salt. The song had become famous quickly for its mix of rock, old and new, and finished with Sia's 'Titanium.' It represented everything Remington LaRoché stood for, and people had loved it.

"I absolutely loved that mix!" Phoenix enthused. "I have it on my iPod."

Memphis pressed her lips together, blushing even as she smiled, her eyes looking down at the floor.

"Didn't you do a movie score for that movie Legend Azaria did too? The really dark stuff?"

"Yes, that was me too," Memphis said, sounding far from egotistical.

"Damn, I had no idea," Phoenix said. "Hey, I have your CD, it was really good."

Memphis scrunched up her face as she breathed out through her nose in a near snort. "Thanks. BJ was pretty pissed I didn't want to do any more, or tour to support it."

"Why didn't you?" Phoenix asked, sensing something in her tone.

Memphis shrugged avoiding Phoenix's gaze. "Not really into fame, that's all."

Phoenix nodded. "Oh, I get that."

"Really?" Memphis said, her tone completely sincere. "Everybody else thinks I'm nuts…" she muttered, partially under her breath.

"Being famous means people think they know you, and they don't, but thinking they know you means they can hurt you."

Memphis' head snapped up, her eyes widening, an odd half smile on her lips. "Yeah, exactly."

Phoenix looked back at the slightly built blonde in front of her, noting the posture that was turned inward. And then it clicked: this was the girl that had been rescued from a cult. Holy shit! Phoenix simply nodded.

"Well, I totally dig your stuff," Phoenix said a few minutes later. "I even have the soundtrack to *For the Telling*, just because I liked it so much."

"Wow," Memphis replied, looking truly surprised, "thanks, that's really cool to hear."

Phoenix inclined her head as they continued their workout. An hour later, they were sweaty and breathing heavily as they sat down on the mat together, guzzling water and mopping their faces with towels.

"So, I'm doing a DJ gig down in San Diego in a couple of weeks," Memphis said.

"For Pride?" Phoenix asked.

"Yeah, how'd you…"

"I'm from San Diego, hit up Pride every year since I came out," Phoenix replied.

"Oh, cool… Well, if Kai would let you off, would you wanna come?" Memphis asked. "A bunch of my friends are heading down, some of us are riding motorcycles. I noticed you ride." She nodded toward the Triumph sitting out on the curb in front of the gym.

Phoenix smiled, feeling lucky to be included. "That'd be great."

"Cool," Memphis said, smiling, feeling like she'd found another person that understood her.

Chapter 3

"I must be losing my hearing on this tour, I thought you said you are going to protect Billy Montague?" Xandy asked.

At her end of the line, Quinn dropped her head, grinning. "You heard me right."

"Seriously! Billy Montague?"

"Yeah, BJ asked me himself."

"And if BJ asked you to jump off a cliff…" Xandy murmured.

Quinn laughed outright. "Babe, I need the money if you want to build onto the house."

"I said I could pay for that!" Xandy exclaimed.

"And I said you can pay half," Quinn replied smoothly. It was a long-standing discussion between them. Even though Xandy made much more money than Quinn did, Quinn refused to let Xandy pay for everything. Quinn knew it was her pride, but she wasn't willing to let it go. She didn't want to be a kept woman, it wasn't her style.

"But if it means protecting Billy Montague…"

"Xan, she's learned her lesson with all of us. After that Memphis incident in Texas, she got better, remember?" A while back there had been an incident between Memphis and Billy. Billy was being impossible and Memphis got fed up and stormed out of the tour venue. While on her rage walk, Memphis encountered a preacher who made the mistake of trying to 'save her soul,' who she punched, which landed her in jail. The incident sparked off a series of events that endangered Memphis' life. Billy had received a fairly rough talking to by Remington, someone most people weren't brave enough to mess with. It had affected Billy's attitude the rest of the tour.

Xandy sighed on her end of the line. "Okay... I'm not going to say I like it, but I know that if anyone can protect Billy, it's you."

Quinn smiled. "Now yer just tryin' ta make up." Her Irish accent became thicker in her humor. Xandy laughed, a warm happy sound, and Quinn found that she missed the beautiful blonde more than she'd let herself realize. She sighed loudly. "How many more months?" she asked wistfully.

"Just two," Xandy replied softly.

"Yeah..." Quinn's voice trailed off with the melancholy that threatened to drape itself around her. Rolling her shoulders, as if mentally throwing off the feeling, she settled back on the bed, staring up at the ceiling. "Oh, some of us are heading down to Pride in San Diego next month."

"Wow, okay, what inspired that?" Xandy was relieved at the change in subject. Her heart had started to ache at the sound of Quinn's voice—she could sense the Irishwoman's sadness, and she knew if she let herself travel too far down that path, it could be a problem.

"Well, Memphis is spinning down at a club called Gossip Grill during Pride, so..."

"So you and Remi are going to keep an eye on her." Xandy finished Quinn's statement with a smile.

"Yeah." Quinn smiled, oddly comforted that her girlfriend knew her so well. "Some of the others are going too."

"Like?"

"Like Jet, Sky, Devin, Cody, and Dak, and this new kid, Phoenix, that Kai's training."

"Wow, some newbie gets to go?"

"Memphis invited her personally."

"Well, then she must be okay," Xandy replied. Memphis was the group's divining rod when it came to people. If Memphis liked and trusted someone, she was always right about them. It had proven true time and time again. She just had a knack about people.

"Yeah, she seems like a nice kid. Cody and Dak like her too. They kind of sense a kindred spirit there."

"Really..." Xandy said, now quite curious about the newcomer. "What's her story?"

"We don't know much yet, other than she's training with Kai to try to pass some agility test to be a smoke jumper."

"A what?"

"Apparently they're firefighters that parachute into dangerous situations to fight fires."

"Oh, so she fits right in," Xandy said with a laugh.

"Pretty much," Quinn quipped.

***

"He's so tiny!" Memphis marveled as she held Bob the opossum.

Phoenix grinned. "Do you want to feed him?"

Memphis looked like a kid as she glanced at Phoenix. "Can I?"

"Sure"—Phoenix proffered the syringe full of food—"just use this... put it right there at the side of his mouth."

Memphis did as she was told and Bob started to eat hungrily. The sound engineer exulted in watching the tiny animal eat. "This is so cool!"

"Wow, he just really goes for it, doesn't it?" Kai enthused with a wide smile.

"Oh yeah, they don't know much else at this point," Phoenix replied. "Feed me, keep me warm, let me snuggle right under your chin there while you're trying to sleep…" She rolled her eyes.

"So adorable…" Kieran, Memphis' wife, murmured.

"He really is," Phoenix said, her look softening as she watched the tiny marsupial.

"What do you think happened to his mom?" Kieran asked.

Phoenix shrugged. "Hard to say, she might have been attacked by a cat, or something else."

"Maybe hit by a car?" Memphis supplied.

"No." Phoenix reached down to scratch under Bob's chin affectionately. "These little guys don't usually leave Mom's pouch till they're about this age, or a little older… Mom getting hit by a car would have killed him too. So his mother must have been killed by something else, and he crawled out of her pouch in desperation."

"Oh God, that's so sad…" Kieran frowned.

"Well, it happens, and at least he's doing good now," Phoenix replied.

"True." Memphis nodded. "So are you going to bring him to Pride? Or will he be ready to go back into the wild by then?"

"No, he needs to stay with me for a while longer than that, they don't usually leave Mom until around five and a half months, so… I'm gonna rig up something, a pouch of sorts, to keep him in on the ride down. I'll just have to smuggle him into the hotel room."

"Cool! You'll have another traveling companion," Memphis said, smiling.

"Chick magnet," Phoenix said with a wink.

"Ah-ha!" Kieran exclaimed, laughing.

***

"Are you seriously coming at me on the straight away?" Jet threw up a hand in a gesture to Cody as she sped by on her on her mom's Ducati Superleggera. "That was mine you know!" Gunning the engine of her own motorcycle, Jet took off after the other woman. She could hear laughter in her helmet speaker, and then the call of "Bangarang!" from the others in the Lost Bois group.

"Don't be a poor sport, Jet!" Dakota crowed from her bike as she caught up to Jet.

"All of you behave, or I'm calling your moms!" Quinn called from the radio in her car.

"Ohhhh…" came a number of replies.

"And coming up on the right…" Harley muttered bad temperedly.

"Don't be whiney cause you don't have your jet car!" Dakota called.

"And why didn't I drive my Z?" Harley sighed.

"'Cause, babe, you needed the air on your helmeted face," Shiloh told Harley over the radio from Devin's Hummer.

"How long does it take to get to San Diego?" McKenna asked, glancing over at Devin.

"At this rate," Devin replied, grinning as another motorcycle, a Harley ridden by Memphis, zipped by the others, "not long!"

Riding along in general silence was their newest misfit Phoenix, who wasn't familiar enough with everyone to dare racing or try to compete. She was, however, listening to all the goings-on as she rode her restored Triumph Bonneville T120.

They'd managed to secure a block of rooms at a hotel in La Jolla.

"This might keep some of us out of trouble," Remington had said, narrowing her eyes at Cody, Jet, and Dakota.

All three women were wise enough to assume a completely innocent look, not that it convinced anyone.

Phoenix made a point of checking on Bob, who'd ridden down with the ladies in the Hummer.

"He's fine, we kept an eye on him," Devin told Phoenix with a wink.

Phoenix laughed. "Thank you."

The valets at the Hotel La Jolla stood mouths agape as the vehicles pulled up the drive. As women began taking off helmets, and piling out of the cars, all varying degrees of tough-looking butch and very femme were represented.

There was a bit of a ruckus as Remington was recognized, and there were whistles of appreciation for the Shelby. Quinn handed one man the keys, telling him in no uncertain terms not to scratch it.

"Fhuair mi e?" she said in Gaelic. "Got it?"

"Ma'am!" the young man responded, looking like former military, sensing Quinn's military background and knowing an order when he heard one.

Remi shook her head at the redheaded Irishwoman. "Always so forceful, telman difisil." Calling Quinn "so difficult" in Creole.

"Hey, it's the new baby..." Quinn replied.

"Yeah, yeah," Remi replied, rolling her eyes.

In the lobby chaos ensued as seven rooms were registered and everyone made their way to the elevators. It took a few elevator rides and another hour for everyone to settle in and then meet in the bar at the top of the hotel for drinks.

Quinn and Remington, who were bunking together, made it to the bar first, and took over an entire section of the restaurant area.

"They're where again?" Quinn asked shaking her head. "Can't ever keep it all straight."

"I think they're in Raleigh tonight and then Atlanta," Remington replied, leaning back to catch the bartender's eye, holding up a finger for another round.

"At least they're headed in the right direction."

"Back this way?" Remington asked, her dark eyes sparkling with humor.

"Too right!" Quinn exclaimed.

"What's right?" Jet asked as she pulled up a chair.

"Our girls headed back toward California," Remi put in.

Jet nodded, signaling the waitress. "Don't know how you two deal with that all the time."

"Deal with what?" Cody asked as she approached with McKenna.

"Never mind," Quinn said, rolling her eyes.

"You drinking Tequila?" Cody asked Jet.

"You know it," Jet replied, leaning back.

"Make it two," Cody told the waitress. "Kenna, what are you drinking?"

"I'll just have white wine."

"Lightweight," Jet muttered.

"Alcoholic," McKenna countered with a wink.

"Behave," Quinn put in, holding her hand up as Jet leaned forward intent on a smart rejoinder.

Jet pressed her lips together in subdued humor and sat back.

"See how well trained she's getting?" Cody couldn't help but say.

"I'll show you trained," Jet retorted.

"Ede m' bondye…" Remington muttered, saying "help me God" in Creole.

"Got that right," Quinn said, shaking her head. "Don't make me rack yer heads together," Quinn told Jet and Cody.

"Who's getting a head racking?" Harley asked as she and Shiloh joined the group.

"The brats," Remington put in.

Everyone laughed. When Dakota and Jazmine joined, the jokes began to fly. Skyler and Devin arrived shortly thereafter, which only added to the festivities.

The party was really getting going when Phoenix finally got to the bar. She'd fed Bob and made sure he would be fine for a few hours. By then the group was discussing changing venues.

"Isn't Memphis over at Gossip Grill at this point?" Quinn asked.

"Yeah, she's there checking out their sound system for her set tomorrow," Remington replied.

"We could head over and check the place out," Jet suggested.

"So where is it?" Skyler asked.

Everyone turned and looked at Phoenix. By this time everyone knew that she'd grown up in San Diego.

"Whoa!" Phoenix exclaimed, holding up her hands when she realized everyone was looking at her. "I just turned twenty-one this year… I've never been to a bar before…"

"Uh-huh…" Jet muttered.

"Hey, some of you are frigging cops!" Phoenix replied, laughing.

"I'm not," Quinn said.

"Me either," Remington replied.

"We are," Jet and Cody said in unison.

"I'm just a hacker," Harley said.

"You're not *just* anything, babe," Shiloh told Harley with a wink.

"So, where is it?" Jet asked Phoenix with a pointedly raised eyebrow.

"In Hillcrest." Phoenix sighed in defeat. "I may have been there a couple of times…"

"Couple dozen, I'm betting…" Cody muttered.

Twenty minutes later, everyone was assembled at the front of the hotel ready to head over to Hillcrest. What seemed like a fleet of Uber vehicles arrived to take them to the bar. It was a Thursday night, so the bar wasn't very crowded when they arrived. Phoenix was greeted by the doorman, who winked at her and said, "Legal now?" as she handed him her license.

"Uh…" Phoenix stammered, but the doorman only laughed and waved her through.

The rest of the group followed, but not before the doorman stopped Remington and Quinn, excitedly shaking their hands. Remington inclined her head gratefully to the man as he enthused about her fighting abilities. Quinn was at a loss as to the man's excitement with her.

"I saw you on YouTube a while back," the young man said. "White Knight and all."

"Christ…" Quinn rolled her eyes, still embarrassed by her accidental fame. She'd been filmed protecting her then charge, Xandy Blue, in a street fight in Belfast and then later as she drank shots and was toasted by many at a local pub singing the Disturbed anthem "The Vengeful One." The video had been a YouTube sensation, and Quinn was labeled Xandy's White Knight. It only stepped up when her subsequent romance with Xandy was made public when Quinn had rescued Xandy's niece from a tornado-ravaged house. Quinn was constantly recognized for her heroics and term "White Knight" had stuck. It drove her crazy.

Inside, the group watched as a girl with flaming red hair nearly launched herself over the bar to greet Phoenix. The girl peppered Phoenix with kisses when Phoenix leaned in to hug her.

"Guys, this is Jenny." Phoenix introduced everyone in turn.

There were hellos all around and drinks were subsequently ordered as they settled at a long table to the side of the bar.

"Interesting girl," Cody murmured to Phoenix, nodding toward Jenny as Phoenix edged over to bump hips with the younger woman.

"Yeah," Phoenix said, with an embarrassed smile, "she's a bit wild, but nice enough."

Cody gave Phoenix as sideways look. "Nice enough for what?"

"Oh, no…" Phoenix replied, shaking her head, "never went there with her."

"No?" Dakota asked from next to Cody; she'd been listening in.

"Nope," Phoenix said, shaking her head, "she's a bar bunny, not my thing."

Dakota nodded slowly, her eyes flicking to Cody, who just shrugged.

"So deep meaningful relationships then?" Dakota asked.

Phoenix looked back at the contractor, seeing a faint light of humor dancing in her eyes. "Well… no… but not into hit it and quit it either."

"What are we talking about?" Jazmine joined the conversation, noting the devilish look in her girl's eyes.

"Nothing," Phoenix replied, still a bit daunted by the redhead Dakota was with. Jazmine Collette was an incredibly hot dancer, and Phoenix had no idea what one did to get with a woman like that. She found herself tongue-tied whenever the woman addressed her.

"Well, it seems that Phoenix here"—Dakota put her hand on Phoenix's shoulder—"doesn't just hit it and quit it."

"Oh someone with a conscience, how novel," Jazmine said, winking at Phoenix.

"I, well... not... I mean..." Phoenix stammered. "Damn it, I need another drink." With that she got up and walked over to the bar.

It was at the bar that she bumped elbows with a blast from the past. She was jostled and turned to apologize, but stopped as the person spoke.

"Robin?" the woman said.

"Holy shit! Mouse?" Phoenix exclaimed in her shock even as she moved to hug the other woman.

"Still with that, huh?" the woman said, smiling as they parted. "Wow, you've changed!"

The woman stood a few inches shorter than Phoenix's five-foot-six frame. She was very small in stature and build, as she always had been, which was why Phoenix had always called her Mouse. Her real name was Michelle.

"I'm sorry," Phoenix said, trying to adjust her mind. "Wait, how... why are you here?"

"I could ask you the same question, but just call me gay adjacent." Michelle cleared her throat. "My sister..."

"Oh, wow..." Phoenix said, nodding, "but not you."

"I've been a little curious a few times..."

"Really," Phoenix said, giving Michelle a sly smile.

"Stop it!" Michelle laughed, slapping Phoenix's arm. "I didn't know you were... I mean, you are, right?"

"I am." Phoenix inclined her head. "But one thing, I don't go by Robin anymore," she said hastily as she noticed Cody walking toward her.

"What do you—"

"Phoenix," Cody said, stepping up to them, "this round is on me." Her eyes went to Michelle curiously.

"Phoenix…" Michelle said, her voice reflecting the 'oh my' look on her face. Phoenix rolled her eyes, then gave Michelle a stern 'shut up' look.

Cody looked between the two women, trying to figure out what was going on between them. "Thas what I said…" Cody intoned, letting her voice trail off as she waited for some clarification.

Phoenix stepped into the silence. "Cody, this is Michelle, she was my best friend all junior high. Michelle, this is Cody Falco."

"Nice to meet you," Cody said, smiling even as her eyes flicked back to Phoenix, still trying to unravel the mystery. She extended her hand to the smaller woman.

"You too," Michelle said, thinking that 'Phoenix' had a nice-looking friend.

"Would you like to join us?" Cody asked, gesturing to the large group to the side of the bar.

Michelle followed Cody's gesture and her eyes nearly bugged out of her head. Phoenix had that many friends now? Holy cow!

"I… um… sure, but can my sister join too?" she asked, nodding her head at a blonde standing at the bar just behind Phoenix. It was obvious that Michelle's sister was a few years older than her.

"Of course," Cody said, nodding.

"Great! We'll be over in a minute," Michelle said, her eyes going back to Phoenix.

"Cool, cool," Cody said, then moved to the bar. "Phoenix, you still drinking beer?"

"Yeah, thanks," Phoenix answered, glancing down at Michelle who was pointedly eyeing her now. "Let's go sigh hi to Nicole," she told Michelle.

The reunion with Michelle's older sister, who'd always treated Phoenix like an annoyance, was oddly satisfying for Phoenix. Nicole was completely agog at Phoenix's new appearance. When she'd known the younger girl before, Phoenix, or Robin as she was known then, had been skinny and a brat, but now… hottie central!

"Those are your friends?" Nicole pointed a finger toward Cody and the rest, after Michelle told her they'd be joining them. "Oh my God that's Remington La Roché. She's like a major MMA fighter, you fucking know her!"

"Not really," Phoenix told her. "She's part of the group that came down here. I was invited by the DJ, Memphis."

"Holy shit! She's awesome too!" Nicole enthused. "Let's go!"

The three got their drinks and walked back toward the group. There were introductions all around, but Phoenix could see that Michelle was looking for more answers than she was getting.

"Let's go talk," Phoenix whispered in Michelle's ear.

Michelle nodded and followed her out to the front of the club where it was a bit more private.

"So, when did this," Michelle said, gesturing at Phoenix's appearance, "happen?"

Phoenix shrugged. "High school, got into lifting weights and stuff."

"And the gay thing?"

"Senior year," Phoenix supplied, "but probably always."

Michelle nodded, having had this conversation with her sister years earlier. She had no problem with alternative lifestyles.

"So how've you been?" Phoenix asked.

"Alright, I'm in my senior year at San Diego State."

"Graduated early, huh?"

"Yep, at seventeen."

Phoenix nodded. "You were always the smart one."

"You're smart." Michelle gave Phoenix a narrowed look. "You just don't like people to know it."

Phoenix rolled her eyes. "Yeah, yeah. I went a different way after high school."

"Which way is that?"

"Firefighting."

"Seriously?"

"Yeah, I moved to Redding and got a job with Cal Fire up there."

"So are you living with your grandfather then?" Michelle asked, remembering that she'd lost Phoenix most of every summer because she'd gone to Redding to stay with her grandfather.

"Nah, I'm staying in one of my parents' rentals up there, trying to fix up the place."

"So what are you doing back here then?"

Phoenix smiled, she remembered how direct Michelle had always been. "I'm actually training with Kai Temple, she trained Remington for some of her matches."

"So you're getting into MMA fighting?" Michelle queried incredulously.

This time Phoenix laughed, holding up her hands. "Not hardly! I'm trying to pass the agility test to become a smoke jumper."

"A what?"

"Smoke jumper—it's a specialized firefighter that parachutes into remote locations."

"So you're going to jump out of planes, like you learned with your dad?"

"Yeah." Phoenix smiled, liking that Michelle remembered.

"But into fires?" The incredulity was back.

"Well, yeah."

"So…" Michelle began licking her lips as she widened her eyes, "you're still nuts, huh?"

Phoenix couldn't help but hug her oldest friend. Michelle had been a good friend for three years, and they'd gone through some lousy childhood stuff together. It was really good to see her.

A little while later, back at the table, Memphis took a break from DJing and joined the group. She immediately sized up the newcomers; she liked Michelle quickly. Nicole was a bit of a questionable presence, but not a major concern.

"She seems a bit desperate," Memphis told Quinn and Remi when questioned about Nicole. "Not a bad person, but not completely genuine to me," Memphis said with a shrug. She never saw herself as a great judge of character, but Quinn and Remi trusted her instincts, and she hadn't been wrong yet.

Back at the table, food was being passed around, as were more drinks. Michelle observed the members of the group and found that they were definitely an interesting bunch. It was obvious to her how protective the group was of Memphis. The two scariest women, Quinn and Remington, seemed to keep an eye on the smaller blonde constantly. Michelle wondered why that was. Kieran was the one to satisfy that curiosity.

The two women were in the small bathroom at back of the club and Michelle made a comment about Quinn and Remi being protective.

"Oh yes, they are, I'm glad for it," Kieran said, her English accent still clear even after a couple of years in the States.

"Were they her bodyguards or something?" Michelle asked. Phoenix had reminded her who Remington and Quinn were.

"No, no, well… never officially." Kieran laughed softly. "They just became her champions after everything that happened." Michelle's blank look had Kieran pressing her lips together in consternation. "Suffice it to say that Memphis was being hassled by some nasty people and Quinn and Remi, along with a lot of other powerful people, put a permanent stop to it."

Michelle blinked a couple of times, not sure what to make of that statement. It had her googling Memphis' name. That's where she read the stories of what had happened to Memphis Lassiter, and it made her look at the DJ in a whole other way. The poor girl had been through so much in her life, running away from a cult, being held against her will, and almost killed by their religious obsession. She also read that Midnight Chevalier, the governor elect herself, and a large group, including many of the women standing around the table, had gone after Memphis to get her back.

"Everything okay?" Phoenix edged closer, seeing the way that Michelle was looking at the women at the table.

"I… yes, of course, I was just trying to catch up." Michelle smiled, shaking her head, her look wondrous.

Phoenix gave a quirked grin. "Yeah, they're pretty intense, huh?"

"Amazing is how I'd put it."

Phoenix nodded in agreement. She too had done a little research on the people around them, as well as others in the group that weren't in attendance. They were an amazing group of women.

Chapter 4

Memphis reveled in the feeling of the crowd, enjoying their responses whenever she started a new mix. It amazed her that she'd forgotten how good this part of being a DJ felt, the performance, the connection to the dancers at a club, it was invigorating. She was exalting in that when she suddenly noticed a much older woman standing near the DJ booth. It was apparent from the way the woman was looking up at her that she wanted to talk to her. Suppressing her usual anxiety over talking to strangers, Memphis held up a finger to the woman with a smile, and then set up the next song, mixing it into the last, giving herself a few minutes to break away from the table.

Moving to the side of the booth, she looked the woman over: she had salt-and-pepper hair, still mostly black, held back from her face by a clip, the rest flowing around her shoulders. Her build was very slender, and slightly stooped. She wore a long skirt in a myriad of colors and a black silk blouse. She reminded Memphis of an old hippie. The woman's eyes were dark, but her face lit up with a smile when she saw Memphis leaning down to talk to her. She moved in to place her lips right next to Memphis' ear in an effort to be heard over the thrumming of the music.

"I know this is probably silly," the woman more or less yelled, "but would you maybe be able to play an oldie for a senior citizen?"

Memphis couldn't help but smile. The woman's face was very animated when she called herself a senior citizen, and her dark eyes crinkled at the corners as she smiled back at Memphis endearingly.

"I can give it a shot, what song?" Memphis queried.

"'Sugar, Sugar' by the Archies?" the woman asked hopefully.

Memphis blinked a couple of times, trying to call the tune to mind. Regardless she nodded, smiling again. "I'll definitely try!"

"You'll make my whole day!" the woman yelled back, then she moved away from the DJ booth, and went back to her seat near the side of the dance floor.

Memphis went back to her table and picked up her phone to look up the song, plugging in her ever-present Bose sound-canceling headphones so she could listen to the song. She called a break in her set after the song that was playing, saying she had a special treat for them when she came back. Her eyes strayed over to the lady sitting serenely at the table, and she wondered at the woman. She looked to be much older than the rest of the crowd at the bar, but she decided she needed to make a special effort to fulfill her request.

Quinn walked into the DJ booth with a beer for Memphis. "What's up?"

"Doing a special request," Memphis said, even as she took a drink of the beer and continued to work.

"Oh… kay…" Quinn replied, her eyes widening at the comment.

"Don't be cynical," Memphis told her friend, quirking a grin.

Quinn merely chuckled and walked away.

Twenty minutes later, Memphis signaled her return with the beginning of "Prayer in C" a Robin Schultz remix of a song by Lilly Wood and The Prick. As the beat started, Memphis winked at the woman who'd requested her song.

"This is a special request from a lovely mature lady, I hope you don't mind my version…" As she said the last she mixed in 'Sugar, Sugar.' It was obvious from the reaction of the crowd that they weren't sure what was happening, but then little by little everyone started to catch on and there were yells of "Alright!" and "Wooh!" The woman who'd requested the song smiled so brightly that it brought tears to Memphis' eyes. She could tell the song had a major significance and she was happy she was able to make the woman smile.

At Memphis' next break, the woman was waiting at the booth when she came out.

"That was so nice! Thank you so much!" the woman enthused, taking Memphis' hand in both of hers and squeezing it gently.

"I'm glad you liked it," Memphis said, smiling softly.

"It was wonderful!" the woman replied. "I'm Maggie, and you can't know how happy that made me."

"It was no trouble."

Maggie gave her a sidelong look. "I don't think that's true at all," she drawled, "but it did warm an old lady's heart."

"You have a good night, ma'am," Memphis told her, as she saw Kieran motioning her over.

"You too, sweet pea!" Maggie called after her.

As she watched Memphis walk away, Maggie smiled softly, thinking what an amazing world it was now. Her smile, though, was tinged with sadness as she went back to her table to finish her drink. She watched as women danced, laughed, kissed, and drank and she wondered if any of them knew just how lucky they were. She doubted it.

As the group drove into New York the excitement practically hummed from the inside of the car. They were in New York! Finally! As they crossed the Verrazzano-Narrows Bridge from Staten Island toward Brooklyn they all practically held their breath.

"Can you see the Statue of Liberty?" Carrie asked excitedly.

"Not from this angle I can't," Denny, who was driving, replied despondently. It had been a long drive and he was hungry and tired.

"This is so trippy!" Christopher yelled from the back seat.

"Yeah!" Maggie chimed in, not wanting to be left out.

"How far are we from your aunt's pad?" Carrie could barely contain her jubilation.

The fact was they were all excited; none had been far from Lancaster, South Carolina, their entire lives. New York had been their graduation goal since they were in elementary school. Now the city lay before them and there were so many things they wanted to do! It was an exciting time!

"Not far," Denny replied, happy to be able to say that. His butt was getting numb and all he wanted to do was get out of the car, and not get back into it for at least a day.

"We have so much to see, maybe we should go to the Statue of Liberty now," Carrie anxiously suggested. She was just sure they wouldn't get to see everything.

"No, man, I need to crash for a bit, I'm wasted," Denny replied irritably. He was the only one that was allowed to drive his dad's car, so he'd been doing all the driving, and they'd only stopped once for a fast lunch.

"Aw, don't be a drag!" Carrie was obviously disappointed, but Denny couldn't even muster the energy to argue with her. He continued the drive in stony silence.

In the back seat, Christopher and Maggie exchanged a look. They knew Carrie was getting on Denny's nerves—the truth was, she was getting on everyone's nerves. They were excited to come to New York too, but they also knew that Denny was tired and needed a break. It surprised them that Carrie was being so selfish at that point, but they *wouldn't say anything, because Carrie could be a real brat when things didn't go her way. The last thing they wanted was for her to freak out, it would put a damper on the entire trip.*

A few minutes later they arrived at their destination, a reasonable apartment in Greenwich Village. While Denny went up to the door to ring his aunt to let her know they were there, Maggie and Christopher got out of the back seat to stare around themselves in utter wonder. While the multi-storied, red brick buildings were a wonder to kids who'd mostly seen one- and two-story houses, it was the people that had Christopher and Maggie excited. They were in the epicenter of the bohemian culture. There were girls in long colorful skirts and peasant blouses, boys with bell-bottom jeans and no shirts, just a mass of necklaces hanging down their chests. It was a riot of color and style that neither of them had seen in person before.

"So boss!" Christopher gasped!

"This is going to be such a gas!" Maggie replied.

Carrie, who'd gotten out of the car and run down the street in her jubilance, came running back. "There are so many hunky guys!"

Maggie and Christopher looked at each other, and then over to where Denny stood on the steps of his aunt's apartment building. Had he heard that? Carrie was his girlfriend, had been since third grade. The two knew this could spell trouble. They rolled their eyes and went to help Denny with the bags in the trunk.

By the time many of the group Ubered back to the hotel they were all, in one form or another, drunk or close to it. The Uber drivers found out that these women, even drunk, had class, and they tipped well for the insanity the drivers had to deal with on the way back to La Jolla.

In one car there was an extensive discussion on the merits of Linkin Park versus Disturbed. The driver played along, allowing Memphis to take over his car stereo to illustrate her points. Quinn, Remington, Phoenix, and Kieran played the proper audience.

"I'm telling you, Linkin Park has some really deep lyrics," Memphis insisted.

"Yeah but Disturbed'll kick yer ass!" Quinn argued.

Phoenix enjoyed the heated discussion, sensing that there was no anger involved, and really seeing how much Memphis loved music. The woman had headphones in her ears almost constantly. She also found that she was learning a lot about music, and hearing bands she'd never heard before. She was anxious, however, to get back to the hotel to feed Bob. She was worried she'd been gone too long.

In another Uber, Jet and Skyler were in a discussion about where they should go the next day.

"I'm hitting the beach," Jet declared.

"Are you going to be back for the Stonewall Rally?"

"What time is it at?"

"Like six."

"I should be well baked by then," Jet answered with nod, then poked at Skyler. "You could use some sun yourself, Sky, you're looking rather pale."

"I've been working my ass off, I haven't had time to tan."

"Well, you're on a break this weekend, you should give it a shot. We could grab some drinks, watch the local scenery…" Jet's voice trailed off as she raised her eyebrows suggestively.

"You remember that her wife is sitting right here, right?" Devin queried.

"Well, yeah, who do you think we're going to start with watching?" Jet winked lasciviously.

Skyler and Devin looked at each other and shook their heads, laughing.

"I need to go shopping. La Jolla's got some great stores!" Devin informed them.

"Oh, and there's an awesome breakfast place in La Jolla. We gotta hit that first!" Jet said. "Cat was telling me about it, it's called Richard something or other."

"That narrows it down," Skyler muttered.

"I'll message Cat. Supposedly they have this totally amazeballs coffee."

"Coffee?" Skyler looked perplexed.

"Yeah, it's like some kind of out-of-body experience thing."

"You and coffee…" Devin intoned, shaking her head.

"Well, their food is supposed to be good too. I'll message the rest of the group to see if anyone else is up for it."

"You do that." Skyler leaned back against Devin, feeling the effects of the shots they'd been doing in the last hour at the bar. Devin put her arms around Skyler's shoulders, leaning down and kissing her head.

Back in their room a half an hour later, Devin looked over at her wife as they got into bed. "Are you sure you shouldn't just get some extra sleep tomorrow?"

"Why?" Skyler queried, pulling Devin down into her arms and snuggling her close.

"Because you've been burning it at both ends lately."

Skyler kissed Devin's lips with what quickly turned to passion. Minutes later they were making love and the conversation was over until they lay trying to catch their breath.

"Was that your way of shutting me up?" Devin asked with a raised eyebrow.

"Never." Skyler snuggled closer, sighing. "I know I've been pushing it, I'll get a chance to relax on the beach."

"See that you do," Devin warned her, sounding very much like a mother.

They'd tried to have a child, but it hadn't happened for them with in vitro fertilization. Skyler planned to talk to her brother about donating sperm, but she wasn't sure if he'd be willing.

"Have you talked to Sebo yet?" Devin had apparently been thinking along the same lines Skyler had at that moment.

Skyler sighed, shaking her head. "He's been so busy with his new team, I haven't really gotten him alone lately."

Devin nodded. "You haven't changed your mind, have you?"

Skyler gave her a quelling look. "No, babe, I've just been busy and so has Sebo. Besides, the doctor said we should wait a bit."

"I know," Devin agreed.

It had been a long road, and they'd spent thousands of dollars trying to get pregnant. The shots Devin had been getting had made her hormones rage and they'd ended up in more than one fight. It wasn't something either of them wanted to experience again soon. Skyler had made the suggestion of trying to get pregnant with Sebo's sperm and it had sounded like a good idea. Devin was secretly afraid that Skyler was over the whole idea and had thought that was why she hadn't talked to her brother yet.

"I will ask him, babe, I promise," Skyler assured.

"Okay." Devin kissed Skyler, seeing that her wife was already falling asleep.

***

The morning quiet in the coastal town of La Jolla was broken by the sounds of various motorcycles and the growl of a Shelby Mustang engine. They'd followed each other from the hotel and now found various places to park around the local businesses. Devin, driving her Hummer, managed to find a parking space in front of the Richard Walker's Pancake House. She went inside and informed the young man at the host desk that they'd need a few tables. Phoenix, who'd headed out earlier on to secure a 'babysitter' for Bob with the local wildlife group, thus freeing her up to enjoy herself, met them there.

"For how many?" he asked, doing his best not to stare at the woman in front of him. She was really beautiful with rainbow streaks in her hair. Standing around her were three other women equally beautiful.

"Fourteen." Devin smiled at the young man, seeing his mouth agape at the number she gave him.

"Ah, si." The young man nodded. "Give me just a few minutes."

As Devin, Shiloh, McKenna, and Jazmine waited, the others joined them.

Jet looked around them. "This coffee better be as good as Cat was saying, I'm way too hungover for crappy coffee…"

"Next time don't drink your weight in Casa Noble," Quinn told her.

"Hey, I don't go halfway here." Jet laughed, even as the man walked back up to the front with a stack of menus in his arms.

"Please follow me," he told them, his eyes widening slightly at the number of women now gathered there.

Once they were seated he offered coffee. Most of the group nodded as they turned over the cups on their place setting. The man came back with a steaming pot and poured some for each, and another man followed with tiny pitchers of cream.

Jet, who took no cream or sugar in her coffee, immediately took a sip.

"Holy shit," she exclaimed, "I think I just died and went to Heaven."

"That good?" Quinn asked, as her coffee was poured. She took a drink as well and murmured her agreement. "Bloody amazing!"

One by one the coffee drinkers tried the steaming liquid and there were exclamations of wonder and appreciation all around.

"I just got goosebumps!" Devin even said.

Once the coffee passed the test everyone began looking at the menu. Just then a pretty Latina waitress walked up, smiling at the group.

"Hi, I'm Emily, I'm going to be helping you this morning. How is everyone?"

"Hungover," Jet replied with a pained half grin, "but the coffee is helping, please send more." She held up her now empty cup looking mournful.

Emily laughed, sensing that this was going to be an interesting table, as she signaled Roberto for more coffee.

"Are there any questions about the menu?"

"What do you recommend?" Remington asked.

"Well, my personal favorites are our waffles, but I can never choose." Emily rolled her eyes in a self-effacing look. "So I really love our Fly Me to the Waffle Moon." She pointed to the selection on the menu. "You can pick any four of our waffles and get a section of each. I love the Georgia Pecan and the Bacon waffles."

"Bacon waffle?" Skyler perked up at that. "I'm in!"

"I'm more along the lines of low carb," Remington told the waitress.

Emily canted her head, thinking the woman looked familiar to her, but couldn't figure out why. "We have a lot of egg selections, even a Venice Benedict, which has spinach, mushrooms, and bacon."

"Bleh, vegetables," Cody said from the other side of the table.

"Not everyone can eat like you, Code," Jet told her.

"Look who's talking," Cody replied, giving Jet a comical look.

"What are ya gonna do about it?" Jet challenged.

"My money is on Cody," Dakota put in.

"Ten on Jet," Harley put in.

"Let's not start, kids." Quinn put her hand out to stop the bickering. "It's too early for that," she said, winking at Emily, who suppressed a laugh. They definitely were going to be entertaining.

After their order was finally taken, and they had refills of coffee they began discussing their day.

"Well, I'm going shopping," Devin informed them.

"I'll go with you," Shiloh said.

"Me too," Kieran put in.

"I'm in." McKenna held up a finger, even as she took a bite of her waffle.

"I'll go too." Jazmine smiled. "Dakota owes me a birthday present."

"I what?" Dakota queried, around a mouthful of bacon.

"My birthday present..." Jazmine replied.

"Oh, yeah, sorry, replacement present, got it." Dakota looked repentant immediately.

"Oh shit, what did you do wrong?" Cody asked.

"It was just a thought," Dakota muttered.

"You thought I wanted an old dilapidated house to fix up?" Jazmine queried.

"But it was a perfect Gothic Revival!" Dakota blustered, even as everyone else groaned.

"My friend," Remington began, putting her hand on Dakota's, "a gift is supposed to be for the recipient, not for yourself. Konprann? Understand?"

Dakota pressed her lips together looking guilty, then sighed. "I know…" It was clear that she and Jazmine had already discussed this at length.

"So much to learn, zanmi mwen," Remington told her, calling her "my friend."

"Well, I'm hitting the beach, maybe do some snorkeling. Who's with me?" Jet asked.

"Here," Skyler said.

"Me too," Cody answered.

"I'll give it a try," Dakota said around a mouthful of bacon waffle.

"Guess I'll work on my tan," Harley put in.

"I can show you some good spots for snorkeling and sunbathing," Phoenix, who'd been fairly quiet that morning, put in.

"We'll escort the ladies," Quinn said, glancing at Remington who nodded agreement. "What about you?" Quinn's look fell on Memphis who hadn't spoken up yet.

"I have some stuff to organize for the rally tonight…" Memphis began.

"Come shopping with me, love," Kieran entreated in her English accent. "Maybe we can find you something new for your gigs here."

Memphis looked conflicted, but finally agreed.

When the check came, Memphis grabbed it from Emily.

"What's our share?" Cody asked, reaching for her wallet.

"Yeah, ours too," Dakota said.

"I got this." Memphis held up a hand as she pulled out her debit card.

"No, absolutely not," Remington said, shaking her head as she reached for the check, but Memphis danced out of her reach smiling.

"You all came down here to support me, and I want to treat you all to breakfast, okay?" she said, her blue eyes shining with appreciation.

There were grumbles and quietly expressed complaints, but eventually everyone agreed. When Emily brought back the receipt, Memphis signed it with a flourish, and added a sizeable tip for her. So sizeable that Emily pointed to it, concern clear on her face.

"Ma'am, I think you put two zeroes here by mistake." Emily grimaced, wanting to make sure Memphis was billed correctly.

Memphis gave Emily her warmest, most charming smile. "You had to put up with all of this"—she gestured her hand around to take in her motley group of friends—"you deserve that tip."

Emily laughed softly, shaking her head. "You guys were awesome, I enjoyed serving you."

"Well, you'll likely see us again tomorrow and the next day," Jet said, holding up her cup one more time to be filled. "Just keep the coffee coming!"

Everyone laughed, including Emily who took a pot of coffee from a passing waiter to refill everyone's cups again. "I can give you all to go cups if you'd like…"

"Oh yo, right here!" Cody put her finger up.

"Here too," Dakota chimed in.

When they left the restaurant twenty minutes later they were fully stocked with cups of coffee, and multiple bags of Richard Walker Pancake House coffee to take home. Emily also supplied them with the website address where they could order more.

"Damn, you were right about that place!" Cody enthused, banging Jet on the shoulder.

"It did not disappoint," Dakota agreed.

"It was bloody incredible!" Quinn laughed.

The group walked down the street trying to figure out which way to head to begin their day. Phoenix gestured toward the ocean. "Anyone wanting to hit the beach, we can head this way. There's a place right by the Sunny Jim Cave to rent wet suits and snorkel equipment."

"Sunny who?" Remington queried.

"It's an old smuggler's cave from the early 1900s," Phoenix said, rubbing the bridge of her nose as she squinted against the sun. "It's pretty cool, you can actually go down to it, or swim into it from the ocean side."

"Well, I guess we'll check that out too," Harley said, pulling out her sunglasses.

"Alright, we'll meet you all down there by around one, okay?" Devin said, leaning up to kiss Skyler on the lips, then gave her a pointed look. "Stay out of trouble."

"Who me?" Skyler queried, already grinning.

"Yeah, you," Devin said, then she poked a finger at Jet. "And you don't try to get her into trouble either, buddy!"

Jet just smiled wickedly.

"Oh shit…" Skyler rolled her eyes. "Let's go." She motioned the beach-going group forward and they crossed the street.

Devin, McKenna, and Shiloh shook their heads simultaneously as they watched the bois stroll away.

"That's gonna be trouble, I can feel it," McKenna said.

"Oh yeah," Shiloh agreed.

Devin simply sighed, glancing back at Remington and Quinn. "You two sure you shouldn't go with the troublemakers?"

Quinn canted her head as she watched the bois making their way down the street. "Worst they can do is drown each other."

The rest of the group burst into laughter.

Four hours later at one o'clock, the group met up on the curve of sand known as La Jolla Cove. The girls who'd been shopping sported various bags, and they'd also brought bottles of water for the bois. The group sat on the beach watching the waves and others play as they relaxed for a little bit longer.

When they were done, Quinn stood up. "Okay, who wants to go to the cave from the land side?" Jet, Cody, and Phoenix had gone in from the ocean side, while Memphis and Skyler had stayed on the beach.

A group formed up to go into the cave, while the others wandered around the gift shop. Afterwards they all decided it was time to head back to the hotel to shower and get ready for the rally that night. They decided to have dinner at Cusp, the restaurant on the top floor of the hotel, and set a time to meet up.

There was a fairly rowdy dinner, which had Remington and Quinn reminding the others that they shouldn't get the group kicked out of the hotel with their antics. Afterwards, everyone once again piled into Ubers to make their way to Hillcrest for the Stonewall Rally. Once there, Memphis got to work setting up her equipment, while the others got themselves seats. Little by little the area filled up with people dressed in their rainbow garb and outlandish outfits. Unfortunately, there were also protestors that showed up with their "Repent now!" "God hates fags!" "Gay Pride is a SIN!" signs, chanting horrible things at the rally goers.

"I frickin' hate those morons!" Phoenix growled, eyeing the protestors.

"They're just religious fools," Remington muttered, her eyes on Memphis who was continually glancing over her shoulder at the group. "They're making Memphis nervous though."

On stage, Memphis was just about ready to start spinning music. On one of her surreptitious looks over her shoulder at the protestors, she noticed Maggie, from the bar the night before, standing next to the stage dressed in a rainbow skirt with beads, and all sorts of rainbow accessories. Memphis smiled at her. "What'll it be this time?" she asked with a chuckle.

"How about 'One' by Three Dog Night?" Maggie queried, her brown eyes sparkling with mischief as she looked up at Memphis.

"I'll see what I can do," Memphis replied, once again glancing toward the protestors, her look disconcerted.

"Don't worry about them, sweet pea, we earned the right to be here this night!" Maggie told her, putting her fist up in the air.

Memphis canted her head and a look of curiosity crossed her features. "Were you there? At Stonewall?"

"I was," Maggie said, nodding.

"Would you tell me about it?" Memphis asked, sounding so very young.

"I'd love to!" Maggie exalted. "Play me my song, and I'll tell you my story."

Memphis inclined her head, happy to indulge anyone who'd been at the scene of the Stonewall Riots.

Chapter 5

The group's tour of New York had started off with the usual tourist traps, but by then Carrie and Denny were fighting constantly. It got so bad that Maggie and Christopher decided to go out on their own to explore the city. They made their way to Washington Square Park and enjoyed sitting and listening to musicians play songs of their own, and those of the bands that were slated to play Woodstock a couple of months from then. They grabbed lunch from a street vendor and sat and people watched for a few hours, loving that they didn't have to listen to any more arguing.

At one point, and very effeminate-looking young man in bell bottoms, a Who tank top and flip flops walked by. Maggie noticed that Christopher's eyes tracked the young man, and she pressed her lips together, not sure if she should say something. She'd known that Christopher was into other boys for a while now, even if he hadn't admitted it yet.

"Hey, let's head that way," Maggie said when the man had passed, gesturing in the same direction he had gone.

Christopher almost managed to suppress the excitement in his eyes at her suggestion as he nodded, standing up and brushing off his jeans. He and Maggie wandered in the direction the man had gone. Three blocks or so later they found themselves on Christopher Street.

"Look, it's named after me!" Christopher extolled excitedly.

"Will you looky there..." another voice commented drolly before Maggie could answer. Both Christopher and Maggie turned to see the

young man they'd been following. He twirled a lock of his curly brown hair and stared directly at Christopher. "Where you from, sugar?"

"Uh... Sou... South Carolina," Christopher stammered, never imaging that this young man would be so direct.

"Oh that's so sweet," the young man countered. "Your accent, honey," he explained in response to Christopher's blank look.

"Oh, thank you," Christopher managed.

"Mm-hmm..." the young man murmured. "I'm Jessie."

"I'm Christopher...like the street," Christopher said, pointing up at the sign. "And this is—"

"Your girlfriend?" Jessie interrupted.

"Um, well, no, I mean, not really, we're just friends." Christopher's words tumbled out in his nervousness.

Jessie sauntered over to Christopher, putting a finger to Chris's cheek. "Don't worry, sugar, I don't bite... unless you ask me to!" He laughed uproariously at his own joke, and then gestured further down the street. "You can come on down to my place," he told them, his eyes never lighting on Maggie for more than a second.

Christopher looked at Maggie; it was obvious from the expression on his face that he wanted to follow Jessie, but he was suddenly aware that he was showing a side he'd never expressed before and he wasn't sure how Maggie was taking it. She smiled encouragingly. The relief on Christopher's face was almost painful. It hurt Maggie's heart that he'd been hiding for what was obviously a long time.

They spent the next few hours with Jessie and some of his friends. They hung out on one of the stoops, talking and laughing. There were plenty of uncomfortable moments where Jessie said something decidedly flirtatious and Christopher couldn't figure out how to react, but Maggie could tell he was happier than he'd ever been.

"So you knew?" Christopher queried, still smiling broadly as they walked back to Denny's aunt's apartment later.

Maggie regarded Christopher for a long moment, then shrugged. "Yeah, I figured it was something like that." She rubbed the bridge of her nose. "I mean, how many times have we been in a situation that would normally end in a kiss, that didn't?"

Christopher grinned. "How did you know it wasn't just that your breath stank?"

Maggie's mouth dropped open in shock, and she was preparing a nasty retort when she saw the glint of humor in her friend's eyes. "You big turkey!" She smacked him on the arm as they both laughed. "So, are you going to go back and go to that bar he invited you to?"

"Only if you'll come too."

"I don't want to be a drag," Maggie said, shrugging.

"You won't be!" Christopher insisted. "I need you there. Besides," he said, giving her a pointed look, "what are you going to do? Hang out with Denny and Carrie and listen to them argue?"

Maggie sighed. "True."

"Then it's a date, tomorrow night we'll go."

"Tomorrow night," Maggie agreed.

It was the beginning of a new adventure!

"Okay, those people are really getting on my nerves," Phoenix growled. Her eyes were on the protestors who were currently chanting something about being gay being a sin, holding signs like "God hates fags!" and "You're going to Hell!"

"They get on everyone's nerves, that's what they're trying to do." Skyler leaned over to tell her.

"Well, it's working." Phoenix curled her lips in disgust.

"Tune them out." Jet shrugged. "It's easier."

Phoenix didn't look convinced by the idea. As the music began and the first speaker arrived on stage, the group turned their attention to them. There were three speakers who talked about what the LGBTQ community needed to do for their future. Each member of the group had their own story, and felt the words in very different ways, but everyone left the rally feeling more committed to acts that would better serve their community.

The group waited for Memphis near the side of the stage. She was engaged in a conversation with an older woman. Finally, she walked over to the group, with the woman walking with her and Kieran.

"Hey guys!" Memphis exclaimed excitedly. "I want you to meet Maggie. She was actually at the Stonewall Riots! Can you believe that?"

Remington extended her hand to Maggie. "You were there?"

Maggie took Remi's hand, smiling shyly up at the handsome butch. "I was."

"Then it's an honor to meet you," Remington told her, bowing her head respectfully.

"Oh my…" Maggie breathed, looking enchanted. "You are a handsome one, aren't you?"

Remi pressed her lips together, looking slightly embarrassed by the praise.

"Hi Maggie, I'm Quinn," the Irishwoman said, stepping forward to extend her hand. "Don't mind Remi, she don't know what to do with compliments."

The group chuckled, even as Maggie stared up at Quinn. "You're Irish?"

"Yes, ma'am," Quinn replied.

As each member of the group introduced themselves, Maggie felt rather overwhelmed by so many lovely women.

"They certainly are making lesbians in all shapes and sizes these days!" Maggie exclaimed, fanning herself dramatically.

"Would you care to accompany us to dinner?" Remington asked.

"Oh, I don't know…" Maggie hesitated. "I don't want to be a bother."

"You're not bother at all," Phoenix put in, winking at Maggie, as she stepped closer to the woman. She took Maggie's hand and placed it gently in the crook of her arm. "I'll be your escort."

"Well, in that case!" Maggie enthused, smiling brightly.

As the group strolled down the street, protestors on the same side of the street screamed at them, calling them sinners and telling them they were going to hell.

"I don't believe in hell!" Cody yelled back at them.

In response they were assailed with multiple insults. One came from a rather large woman wearing red-and-white striped shorts and an American flag shirt. She yelled, "Non-believers will burn!"

"Fucking bullies!" Phoenix growled.

"They don't understand," Maggie said, shaking her head sadly.

"They don't want to understand," Jet said.

"Well, we earned this," Maggie said solemnly, so much so that Cody misunderstood.

"Getting screamed at? We earned this?" Cody asked.

"No," Maggie said, shaking her head. "We earned the right to be who we are, no matter what anyone thinks."

They ended up at the very colorful, and very gay friendly, Baja Betty's restaurant and bar, whose motto was "Home Sweet Homo!" While it was a bit of a wait, since the restaurant was one of the most popular in Hillcrest, Memphis and Phoenix managed to charm the hostess into letting Maggie sit with the two of them inside, out of the evening heat and away from the press of bodies.

"So what do you do?" Maggie asked Phoenix with a sly smile. "Besides escort little old ladies, that is!"

Phoenix chuckled, her light eyes sparkling. "I'm a firefighter, ma'am."

"Oh…" Maggie responded, looking impressed, putting her hand on Phoenix's arm. "Tell me more!"

Phoenix smiled widely, covering Maggie's hand with her own. "I joined the fire department at the age of eighteen. I got my wildland firefighter certification last year, and now I'm working on becoming a smoke jumper."

"What does a smoke jumper do?" Maggie's eyes were wide with fascination.

"They parachute into remote fires to fight them."

"Isn't that dangerous?" Maggie's tone was aghast.

"Yes, ma'am, that's why there's very few of them, and only twenty-six women at this point," Phoenix replied seriously.

Maggie added her other hand to hold Phoenix's in both of hers. "You be sure to be careful! That sounds very hazardous to your health!"

Phoenix chuckled, even as she lowered her eyes. "It is," she said, "but it'll be worth it if I can make a difference."

"That's the thing, isn't it?" Maggie replied wisely. "To make a difference…" Her voice trailed off wistfully.

"Well, you were at the flashpoint of history," Memphis said to Maggie. "Being in New York during those crazy times. That must have been something!"

Maggie sighed, nodding gravely. "It was something, alright." Her sullen look belied the difficulty of those times.

"May I come in?" asked a voice from the other side of the hospital curtain.

Maggie glanced up from her place in the chair next to Christopher's hospital bed.

"Yes," Maggie answered.

The woman that stuck her head around the curtain had bright blue eyes—it was the first thing Maggie noticed. She then took in the woman's short sandy-brown hair, with a lock of strands falling over her forehead.

"I'm Danielle," the woman said, extending her hand to Maggie, her blue eyes taking in the bruise to the young woman's face, and the cut on her lip. "What's your name?"

"I'm Maggie, this is Christopher." Maggie gestured to her friend, then looked quizzically back at Danielle. "What can we do for you?"

Danielle nodded to Christopher to acknowledge the introduction, then looked back at Maggie with kind eyes.

"I'm a social worker," Danielle told them, "I understand you two were involved in a bit of a dustup this evening down on Christopher Street."

"We didn't do anything wrong!" Christopher exclaimed, his eyes alight with renewed anger.

Danielle put out a calming hand. "I didn't say you did anything wrong. I just wanted to talk to you two about what happened."

Maggie and Christopher exchanged a worried look.

"What did everyone else say?" Maggie asked cautiously.

Danielle recognized the carefulness and nodded, understanding the girl's hesitation. Christopher Street was a hotbed of tumult in New York. Things were always simmering down there.

"We know that the police raided a club, and that a number of people were arrested."

"My friends!" Christopher gasped, worried immediately.

"It's okay," Danielle assured him. "Most of them have already been released."

"Most," Christopher echoed with a look of disdain. "They weren't doing anything wrong either."

Danielle pressed her lips together in consternation. She understood his upset. "What happened to you?" she asked, her blue eyes on Christopher.

Christopher swallowed convulsively, looking somewhat sick at remembering what had happened. "We'd just left the club," he said, gesturing to Maggie, "when the cops showed up. They chased after us, yelling at us to stop and put our hands up."

Danielle nodded encouragingly. "Did you do as they said?"

"Yes!" Maggie exclaimed, her dismay breaking through. "But they didn't seem to care!"

Christopher's lips trembled as he looked at his friend. "They grabbed me by the hair and threw me down on the ground. I told them I hadn't done anything, but they just kicked me!"

"I was screaming at them to stop, telling them that he hadn't done anything," Maggie told Danielle, tears forming in her dark eyes. "They wouldn't listen! I tried to grab one of them, but he just smacked me in the face and pushed me down too."

Danielle took a deep breath through her nose, blowing it out loudly, her look angry. "That's how your lip got split?"

"Yes." Maggie nodded.

"And they broke your arm?" Danielle asked Christopher.

He nodded, looking very affected by all that had happened that night. In truth, he'd never experienced so much violence in his life. It was extremely upsetting.

Danielle nodded again, writing notes in the pad in her hand. When she finished, she put the notepad in the pocket of her jacket. "Where are you two staying right now? Do you have a safe place to be?"

Christopher and Maggie exchanged a look, surprised by the question. "We're staying with the aunt of one of our friends from school. We're just here for a couple of weeks," *Christopher said.*

"Where are you from?" *Danielle asked.*

"South Carolina," *Maggie told Danielle.*

"Oh." *This information surprised Danielle.* "Well maybe you shouldn't hang out around Christopher Street for the rest of your trip."

"It's still a free country, isn't it?" *Maggie asked sarcastically.*

Danielle looked back at Maggie for a long moment, a slow smile spreading over her face. "It's supposed to be, yes."

"Then we have a right to go wherever we want!" *Maggie snapped.*

Danielle raised her eyebrows at the younger woman's spirit, even as she did her best to hold back her amusement. Finally, she shook her head dolefully. "Yes, you can, but you can also expect something like this"—*she gestured to the arm Christopher held against his chest*—"to happen again."

"That's not fair!" *Maggie exclaimed.*

Danielle shook her head ruefully. "No, it's not." *She then reached into her jacket pocket and pulled out a business card, handing it to Maggie.* "That's my card. Please call me if you two get into trouble again. I'll do my best to help you out." *Her look at Maggie was direct and in her blue eyes Maggie thought she saw sympathy and concern, so she took the card and nodded.*

"Thank you," was all Maggie said.

Eventually the group got their table at Baja Betty's. With a bit of influence from Remington and Quinn, they scored a table at the back of the restaurant in a separate room, so it was a bit quieter. After drinks and food were ordered, members of the group started asking Maggie questions.

"So you were at Stonewall?" Jet queried first.

"I was." Maggie inclined her head.

"That had to be exciting!" Jazmine enthused.

Maggie looked more solemn. "I don't know that exciting is what I would call it."

"What would you call it?" Skyler asked.

Maggie was quiet for a moment, as everyone looked on. "Terrifying, confusing, violent."

As Maggie named the adjectives, members of the group grimaced or shook their heads.

"Were you actually at the Stonewall Inn itself?" Quinn asked.

"Oh yes." Maggie nodded. "We were there. It was such a hot night, I'd swear I could just melt into the pavement on the sidewalk." She fanned herself as she remembered. "The air conditioning in the Stonewall Inn never worked, if they even had it at all." She shrugged. "For that matter nothing really worked, toilets, sinks…" Her voice trailed off as she shook her head. "But it was one of the few places we gays were safe, or so we thought."

"Law enforcement harassed gays a lot in those days," Remington put in.

"Well, not me, really," Maggie said, "because I always looked like a 'girl.'" She said the word with air quotes. "But they were constantly after the boys, especially the cross-dressers. They harassed them regularly, citing some old law from the 1800s called the 'three article rule.'"

"What was that?" Dakota asked.

Maggie waved her hand as if dismissing the law itself. "Some ridiculous law that said a person had to have three articles of gender-appropriate clothing on at all times."

"What the hell?" Harley asked, looking disgusted.

"It was about how you looked," Maggie said, "someone like you"—she pointed at Harley—"with your long hair might be able to pass for straight… Or maybe not," she said when Harley flashed her rainbow underdye by lifting her long white hair. "But someone like you," she said pointing to Dakota, and then to Quinn, "with your short hair, no makeup, masculine-looking clothes, they'd have harassed you."

"Where ya goin', dyke?" the cop asked Danielle as she and Maggie strolled down the sidewalk one evening.

Maggie turned to say something, but Danielle squeezed her hand in warning. "Just keep walking," Danielle whispered.

"I'm talkin' to ya, dyke!" the cop growled, starting to follow them.

Danielle increased her pace, practically dragging Maggie with her. They were almost at the office. If they could just get there…

A hand suddenly reached out, grabbing Danielle's sleeve.

"C'mere! You got your three articles?" the cop snapped angrily, his hand clutching at the material.

Danielle shook off his hand and quickened her pace again. This time the hand came down on her shoulder, harsh and bruising, and clutching harder at the cotton material of the button-up shirt. They were three steps from the Social Services offices. Danielle wrenched away, turning her entire body to get out of the man's strong grasp. The sound of material ripping mixed with the sound of cars on the street. People stopped and stared, but Danielle wasn't about to stop. She practically ran the last three steps, pulling Maggie with her.

Once inside the building, the cop glowered at them, but he knew better than to follow them inside. Danielle leaned against the inside wall, her breathing coming in gasps.

"Are you okay?" Maggie asked, staring up at the other woman sympathetically.

Danielle swallowed convulsively but nodded her head. "I'm okay."

"Why was he after you?" Maggie queried.

Danielle's blue eyes lit on Maggie, her smile soft as she looked at the younger woman. "Because I don't look like regular girls."

Maggie shook her head. She'd come to really care about the social worker, who'd been there for her and Christopher time and time again over the last six months. When it had been time to leave New York, Carrie and Denny were still fighting and on the verge of breaking up. Maggie and Christopher had decided they wanted to stay, claiming that they were going to look into colleges. Instead, they'd both gotten jobs and a very cheap studio apartment. They'd both become fixtures on Christopher Street and, unfortunately, Christopher was regularly targeted by the cops. They'd learned quickly how to avoid trouble, but when trouble found them anyway, Danielle had been Maggie's first call each time. And Danielle had come through for them, getting them out of trouble time and time again.

"But you're not a lesbian, are you?" Maggie asked, her dark eyes wide with innocence.

*Danielle quirked her lips. Was the girl really this naïve? "Well…"
Danielle began, not sure she wanted to destroy Maggie's illusion, but
deciding that honesty was likely the best policy. "Yes, I am."*

*Maggie stared back at her openmouthed, blinking repeatedly. "I…"
she began, not sure what to say at that moment. There were so many
emotions swirling inside her, she didn't know which one to express at
that point. "Wow."*

Danielle chuckled as she moved off the wall. "Let's go upstairs."

*Up in Danielle's small, cramped office, she had to move files off the
one extra chair in the tiny room for Maggie to sit down. "Sorry." Danielle sighed as she sat in her own chair behind the desk.*

"What did that officer mean about three articles?" Maggie asked.

"It's just some stupid rule they have, to prove you're not a crossdresser, you gotta have three articles of clothing that fits your gender."

Maggie gave her a confused look and Danielle sighed again.

*"Like my bra," she told Maggie, reaching in and snapping her bra
strap.*

"Oh…" Maggie nodded. "I get it. That's a drag, and so sleazy!"

Danielle nodded. "But it's the way things are."

Maggie frowned. "They really don't like anyone who's different."

"The fuzz only knows one way," Danielle agreed.

"The fuzz?" Jet queried when Maggie mentioned the term.

Maggie laughed, nodding her head. "That's what we called them back then."

Jet rolled her eyes. "I don't think I'd want to be called the fuzz."

Maggie canted her head. "Are you a cop?"

Jet nodded. "So's Cody," she added, gesturing to her friend.

Maggie looked shocked. "Cops never looked like you two in my day!"

Everyone had a good laugh about that.

"So you didn't know Danielle was a lesbian?" Kieran asked, always interested in people's coming-out story.

Maggie shook her head. "I should have guessed it, but in those days I had so little experience with anything outside of the norm. You grow up in a small town, only ever seeing the same kind of people all the time, you don't really recognize differences." She shrugged. "I did guess that my friend Christopher was gay, though, so I guess that's not always true."

"That was your friend you lived with in New York?" Memphis asked as she grabbed one of the newly arrived chicken wings.

"Yes, I loved him so much," Maggie said, a soft smile on her lips.

"What happened to him?" Kieran asked cautiously, worried it was a sore spot.

Maggie frowned sadly. "He died in San Francisco in the mid-eighties," she said. "AIDS."

Everyone in the group winced. "I'm so sorry," Kieran said, reaching across the table to touch Maggie's hand in condolence.

Maggie nodded, accepting the consideration. "At least he got to live his truth until then."

"And you?" Remington asked.

Maggie smiled, tears forming in her eyes. "My truth took a little bit longer to get to."

***

"So who is this you're hanging out with?" Xandy asked when Quinn called her after dinner. The Irishwoman was sitting on the sidewalk outside the restaurant smoking a cigarette.

"Her name is Maggie," Quinn told her, "she's pretty cool. She was actually at the Stonewall Inn the night the riots started!"

"Wow!" Xandy exclaimed. She'd spent time reading about the Stonewall Riots so she was more prepared to talk about gay rights whenever it came up in interviews, which was regularly. "That must be an amazing story! I'll need to hear all about that when you're not under an insanely loud music speaker!"

Quinn chuckled, glancing above her head. Baja Betty's loved to blare music, that was for sure. "It's Raining Men" was playing at that moment. "We haven't actually heard about that just yet, but she was telling us some of the crazy rules. I'm thinkin' I'm glad I wasn't around America in those days."

"Well, I'm sure Ireland had its issues with gays in those days too."

Quinn rolled her eyes. "Babe, they just barely legalized gay marriage four years ago, so… yeah, I'd say being gay in Ireland has its challenges."

Xandy shook her head at her end of the line. She'd never realized how much discrimination and hate was leveled at the gay community until she'd come out. Suddenly, people who'd known her since she was a baby didn't like her, or thought she was 'sinful.' Fortunately, her only real family, her aunt, had learned to accept her, mostly because her own daughter had turned out to be gay too. It was not easy to be gay in any society—she couldn't even imagine having lived through the sixties and seventies being gay!

When Quinn got back to the table, everyone was debating over dessert. Some wanted to 'drink' their dessert, trying various margaritas that Baja Betty's had in great numbers! Others were getting buñuelos, a wonderful concoction of fried flour tortillas coated in cinnamon and sugar, served with vanilla ice cream.

"Great, Quinn's back!" Memphis enthused. "Maggie is gonna tell us about that night at the Stonewall Inn!"

"Iontach!" Quinn exalted. "Fantastic," she translated when she saw the confused looks she was getting. "Tell on, Maggie!" she encouraged, smiling widely.

Maggie smiled brightly, enjoying the company she was keeping at that moment—so many lovely young people!

"As I was saying earlier, it was so hot that night! And the Stonewall Inn wasn't into air conditioning for their patron's comfort. I couldn't stand to wear much, because everything felt so sticky and suffocating! So I had a mini skirt and a tiny little cami top on, with sandals, that I'd regret later…" Maggie grimaced as she remembered the night so clearly.

Chapter 6

"Can someone just dump some ice on me!" Maggie exclaimed, trying to fan herself with the flyer she'd been handed upon entering the club. She proceeded to sign 'the book' using Marilyn Monroe for the millionth time—no one ever used their real name, who would?

"Don't drink, that'll just make it worse," Danielle, who stood at her elbow, advised.

"But I get flirty when I drink, you like that." Maggie laughed at the look on Danielle's face. A combination of guilt and humor was mirrored in those blue eyes.

"I do like that," Danielle agreed, *"but I also don't want you getting sick because you're dehydrated, so stick to at least a water after ever drink, okay?"*

Maggie smiled as she nodded. She loved that Danielle was so concerned about her. Their relationship was still developing. Maggie had no idea how to be a lesbian, but what she did know was that Danielle made her feel more loved and cherished than any boy ever had. To her way of thinking, something that felt this good had to be right, didn't it?

They made their way to the booths where Christopher and his latest boyfriend sat. In the year they'd been in New York, she and Christopher had started at the local community college. It was the only way their parents would let them stay. Neither of them knew what they wanted to do for a living, but they could take general education classes until they figured it out. Christopher had been through a number of boyfriends—he was so handsome, he caught the eye of many of the men in the community.

"Hi Robert," *Maggie greeted, as she leaned in to hug Christopher.*

"Hello Magpie." *Robert smiled with big teeth. He reminded Maggie of a horse, but he was nice to Christopher, so she figured he was a good guy.*

"Don't call me that!" *Maggie frowned, glancing at Danielle who only laughed.* "That's what Dani calls me; you can't call me that."

"Does it make it less special?" *Christopher queried.* "Aren't you so very special?"

The tone and pitch of Christopher's voice told Maggie that he was drunk, which wasn't a good sign. She and Christopher were underage, and shouldn't be drinking at all, but to be very obviously drunk wasn't wise.

"Are you drunk or high?" *Maggie raised an eyebrow at her friend.*

"I'll never tell!" *Christopher chimed, laughing at his own perceived hilarity.*

Maggie exchanged a concerned look with Danielle. They were always hyper-aware of the cops that could burst in at any moment. The last thing they wanted was to call attention to themselves. Maggie watched Danielle lean over to talk to Robert. His lips twitched, and Maggie could tell that the older man didn't like being told what to do, but he finally nodded.

Robert got up from the table and went to the bar. Maggie watched him. He was one of the more masculine-looking men Christopher had dated. He wore jeans and cowboy boots, and a nice button-up shirt. Christopher, on the other hand, had taken up an effeminate persona; she knew he was being influenced by other gay boys he hung around with. Christopher was always excited about a new silk shirt, or pair of hip hugger pants. He frequently tied his shirt tails high up on his torso and walked like a runway model. Maggie thought it was wonderful that he had found himself in New York, but she worried about him constantly with the way the police treated gays, especially men.

"Here, sweetie," Robert said, handing Christopher a glass of water as he sat back down at the table. It was easy to see from Robert's tension that he wasn't sure how Christopher would take the not too subtle hint.

"What am I supposed to do with this?" Chris asked.

"Just drink it, baby, it's so hot in here, I don't want you to get sick," Robert offered gently.

Fortunately, Christopher liked being taken care of, just as Maggie did, so he gave Robert a cute, sweet smile and drank the water. Maggie could feel Danielle relax next to her.

Later in the evening a dark-haired woman with a dusky skin tone walked by the table, stopping to talk to Danielle. As the two chatted, Maggie quietly checked out the woman. She was far from feminine, but still very beautiful. She wore her hair short, and no makeup that Maggie could detect. She was dressed in a sharp-looking suit that fit her to perfection.

"Maggie," Danielle said, touching her elbow to bring her out of her study of the woman, "this is Stormé DeLarverie, she's big in the movement."

Maggie smiled up at the handsome woman, taking her extended hand.

"Tre piti," Stormé said, turning Maggie's hand, then leaning over to cavalierly kiss it softly on the back.

Danielle laughed at Maggie's awed look. "Stormé is from New Orleans, and always the flirt!"

Maggie laughed even as a blush creeped up her cheeks.

"Such a pretty little one," Stormé said, before moving on to speak to other people in the club.

"Stormé is a heavy hitter in the gay movement, she's always trying to start some kind of trouble..." Danielle said. It was clear to Maggie that she admired the other woman a great deal.

It was nearly midnight when there was a ruckus up at the front of the bar. Maggie heard someone yell "Raid!" which terrified her, but there really was nowhere to go. Everyone knew that the manager of the club always kept all of the doors locked.

Danielle grabbed Maggie's hand and stood up, pulling her out of the booth as she did.

"Just put your hands up, and don't say anything," Danielle told her. She put her hands up above her head as people around them called out and screamed.

Maggie did as she was told, but watched as police officers roughed up many people in the club. She watched as one drag queen, known as Lula, started to argue with an officer. The officer took his billy club and hit the queen square in the face. Blood spurted from Lula's nose, and she bent over. The cop kneed her in the jaw, calling her a "faggot."

"Oh god..." Maggie breathed, starting to tremble from head to toe.

"It'll be okay, just don't argue or show any kind of aggression," Danielle whispered.

The officer who'd hit Lula wiped the blood off his billy club with Lula's yellow dress, then moved to another man in the room.

"You faggots know you don't belong in here!" he called. "You dirty fucks! You make me sick!"

"You make us sick," Christopher muttered, unfortunately loud enough for the cop to hear.

"What was that, you little faggot!" the cop said, moving to Christopher, billy club at the ready.

"He didn't say anything," Robert said, stepping forward.

Without warning, the cop swung the billy club up hitting Robert in the side of the head savagely. Robert doubled over, grabbing his head that was now bleeding profusely.

"If I want to hear from you, faggot, I'll let you know!" the cop yelled.

Christopher bent to help Robert, receiving a kick to the face from the cop.

"Stop!" Maggie couldn't help but cry at seeing her friends so brutely attacked.

"What's your problem, baby dyke?" the cop sneered.

"Nothing, sir!" Danielle said, grabbing Maggie's hand and pulling her back, shifting protectively in front of the smaller girl.

The cop's lips curled in disgust. "What did you say, ya fuckin' rug muncher?"

Danielle lowered her eyes to the floor, as she shook her head. "Nothing, sir."

Maggie watched in barely leashed terror, afraid she was about to see the man hurt Danielle too. Fortunately, another patron inserted himself into the scene.

"What's the problem, copper?" the man said, throwing a penny at the officer.

The officer turned on him, and Maggie was able to check on Christopher. His lip was bleeding, so was his nose. She grabbed some napkins off a nearby table.

Slowly but surely, everyone in the bar was ushered outside. Many of the people from the bar were circulating outside as the police hauled off many of the drag queens and a few of the gay men. People from the neighborhood had come down to the street, woken by the police sirens.

Maggie, Danielle, and Christopher helped Robert out of the club; he was still feeling very dizzy from the hit to the head he'd taken.

"We should probably get him to the hospital," Danielle was saying, just as the cops led Stormé DeLarverie out of the club in handcuffs.

Maggie heard Stormé saying something about the handcuffs being too tight, then the police officer turned and wailed on the dark-haired lesbian.

"Come on..." Danielle pulled at Maggie's arm sensing things were getting bad.

Maggie was just turning to follow Danielle when she heard Stormé yell, "Why don't you do something?"

There was a sudden surge in the crowd, and Maggie felt Danielle's hand dragged off her arm by people pushing forward. She started hearing people yelling and glass breaking, and realized people were hurling bottles towards the cops, which unfortunately she was very close to at that point. Doing her best to duck down, Maggie tried to get through the crowd, but they just seemed to press closer together. She thought she heard Danielle call her name, but she couldn't see the other woman.

"Wait! Please!" Maggie cried out, as someone was pushed from the crowd, and stumbled into her, knocking her down. "Please!" she screamed again, terrified suddenly that she'd be trampled by the angry crowd.

Someone beside her picked her up off the ground with strong hands. She turned to see that Robert had pushed through the crowd to get to her. He lifted her up in his arms, and made his way through the throng of people, getting them to the side near the wall of the Stonewall Inn.

"Where's Dani and Chris?" Maggie worried.

"I don't know, we got separated!" Robert told her.

Maggie did her best to look around: police were doing their best to hide behind and beside the patrol cars. People were screaming "Pigs! Coppers!" A brick sailed by, striking the windshield of one of the police cars, and the crowd seemed to surge forward again.

"We gotta get outta here!" Maggie said. The situation was becoming more dangerous and she was worried about Danielle.

Glancing up, she could see that Robert was watching the crowd. He was fisting his hands, and clearly wanted to join the fighting. She couldn't blame him, there was still blood seeping from the side of his head. Police officers were so vicious to the gay community, calling them names and treating them like animals to be put down like dogs. As she watched, Robert leaned down and picked up a brick that had fallen near his feet. He held it in his hand for a long time, his mouth working with his barely held anger.

Maggie reached out a hand, touching him on the hand that held the brick. He turned his head to look at her, his eyes blazing.

"They can't keep doing this to us," he told her, conviction in his voice. "It needs to stop." With that he lifted the brick and threw it in the direction of the police and started joining the chanting. "Fag Power!"

There were other cries of "Liberate the Bar!" and "We're the Pink Panthers!" There was also singing and carrying on as the assault on the officers continued. Maggie did her best to move through the crowd, but found herself on the edge of the fray, when she saw a drag queen hit a police officer in the head with her purse. Maggie couldn't help but yell, "Power to you sister!" caught up in the moment.

By the time she finally made it through the larger part of the crowd, she feared she would never find her friends. She sat down on the curb away from the crowd. That's where Danielle found her half an hour later.

"There you are!" Danielle cried as she leaned down to hug Maggie.

"Where's Christopher?" Maggie asked, looking around them. The crowd seemed to be growing, not diminishing.

Danielle sighed, shaking her head. "He ran off after grabbing a few bottles from the trash can. Hopefully he doesn't get himself arrested." She looked around them, and Maggie couldn't miss the proud smile that spread across her face.

"You're digging this, aren't you?" Maggie asked.

Danielle looked down at her, tears in her eyes. "I am totally digging this, yeah."

They both felt they were on the verge of something great, but it was terrifying at the same time. They were sure shooting would start any minute and that many of their friends and community members could be killed.

Later, Danielle and Maggie were still sitting on the sidelines; Maggie refused to leave without her friends. At nearly four in the morning, Christopher came running over to them, no longer wearing a shirt or shoes, the elation on his face indicative of how he was taking the situation.

"Come on!" he yelled at the two of them. "The cops have barricaded themselves inside the Stonewall! We're gonna burn the place down!"

"What the—" was all Danielle had time to get out before Christopher ran off back toward the bar.

"Did he say they're going to burn the bar down!" Maggie screamed standing up.

"That's what he said," Danielle confirmed. "This is going to be bad. If they kill those cops, we'll be annihilated!"

"I have to stop him!" Maggie ran in the direction Christopher had gone. She heard Danielle scream her name, but she didn't stop. The last thing she wanted was for Christopher to be killed in the middle of this mess.

Pushing her way through the crush of bodies, she could hear people calling for "Sticking the pigs!" It spurred her on and as she made her way toward the windows of the Stonewall Inn, she could see the yellow-orange glow of a fire starting.

She looked left and right for Christopher, trying desperately to spy him in the crowd so she knew where to head, but it was useless. There were so many people yelling and carrying on. She could smell the smoke from the fire, and the terror she was feeling was making her feel lightheaded. She felt pain in her feet and realized they were bleeding, cut from the many broken bottles lying in the street. Her sandals were no protection against the glass.

When she finally broke through the crowd, she was near the front doors of the Stonewall Inn. She watched as a few young men used a parking meter they'd somehow gotten ahold of to attempt to ram the front doors of the Inn. The fire was now burning the wood that had been put up in the windows and people were using lighter fluid to set fire to anything they thought would burn.

Maggie could hear screams and shouts from inside. Someone yelled, "There are people in here!"

Someone next to Maggie shouted, "We're people too, you fucking pigs!"

She couldn't argue with that. The police had been so brutal with so many homosexuals in the neighborhood, they'd never had it turned on them. Maggie knew, though, that Danielle was right—if police officers were killed law enforcement would come down on the gay community like a hammer.

Maggie had just seen Christopher and screamed his name, when she heard the rumble of trucks down the street. She saw the big black trucks with "POLICE" on the side and knew this would be the riot police. Things were about to get worse! Maggie watched as Christopher and a few of his friends looked toward the vehicles. Many of the rioters turned as helmeted officers jumped down out of the trucks, took their shields and billy clubs, and formed a line the entire width of Christopher Street.

Suddenly, Christopher was beside her, practically jumping up and down. "Come on! We're going to pull a sneak attack!" He grabbed her hand and started running. Maggie had to run to keep up with him.

Many other young men were running with them, heading down Christopher Street away from the police. That part relieved her, but then they turned, and Maggie knew what they were doing: they were going to come up behind the cops. She yanked her hand out of Christopher's and stopped running. Christopher stopped and looked at her like she was insane.

"What are ya doing?" Christopher yelled.

"We can't attack the cops!" Maggie hollered back at him. "That's crazy! We'll get killed!"

"They're killing us all the time, Mags!"

Maggie shook her head with tears in her eyes. "I can't do this."

"Well, I can!" Christopher told her, then turned and ran after his friends.

Maggie turned around and started walking back the way they'd come, crying the entire way. As she rounded the corner, she had to step back against the wall of the nearest building. Smashing herself against the wall to keep from being run over as the rioters surged away from the cops who were now beating their billy clubs on their shields as they marched down the street, intent on stopping the riots altogether.

Someone who was backing up stumbled into her and knocked her down. She fell to the ground, crying out as the person landed on her ankle. The person who'd knocked her down got up and kept running. Unfortunately, she was now in the way of others running. People stumbled over her, kicking her in the ribs and arms as she did her best to shelter her head.

Once again, she was saved by a strong pair of hands lifting her up. She smelled perfume and looked into the brown eyes of one of the drag queens who frequented the club. Yellow feathers and gold sequins shimmered and winked as she set Maggie down her feet near the wall.

"Sadie's got you, honey!" She winked, making a kissing sound with her red jam-slicked lips.

"Thank you!" Maggie cried. She lunged forward to hug Sadie, catching her near the middle—she was a good six feet tall, and even taller in the gold heels she wore.

"There, there, little one," Sadie soothed, patting Maggie gently on the back. "You be safe!" she said, and smiled a wide, bright smile. Then she disappeared into the crowd.

Maggie hugged the wall as she did her best to move away from the rioters and the Stonewall Inn. It was six a.m. before she entered the apartment she was currently sharing with Danielle.

Danielle rushed forward, hugging her close. "Thank God you're okay!"

Maggie accepted the hug wearily. "Have you heard from Christopher?"

Danielle shook her head. "Sorry, honey."

Maggie drew in a deep breath tried to hold back tears as she nodded. "I hope he's okay."

Danielle nodded in agreement, but she didn't want to offer too much hope. She'd heard what Christopher and his friends were doing, and she wasn't sure how that was going to go. At the very least he might end up in jail, but it was the worst-case scenario she was worried about.

"Was he okay?" Quinn asked.

They'd all listened to Maggie's recounting of that night with fascination. Ice cream had melted, drinks had gone un-drunk. They were all so mesmerized imagining that night.

Maggie smiled. "He got himself arrested, but they let him go the next day. They had bigger issues to deal with from the gay community at that point."

"Riots?" Remington asked knowingly.

"You betcha!" Maggie enthused. "We even got help from the Black Panthers if you can believe it! They had been fighting suppression for so long, they wanted to come help. It was a wonderful time of change!"

"Did you participate?" Cody asked.

Maggie smiled, nodding her head. "But only the more peaceful ones. Danielle wouldn't let me go if it sounded like there was going to be trouble."

"She took care of you…" Devin sighed wistfully.

"Yes, she did," Maggie agreed. "There were four days of protests and, believe me, the papers weren't nice about how they reported on it."

"What did they say?" Jet asked.

"Oh, one of them called us protestors the 'forces of faggotry.'"

"Charming," Remi said, curling her lips in disgust.

"Another paper headline, I think it was the *New York Daily News*, read 'Homo Nest Raided, Queen Bees are Stinging Mad!'"

Many at the table shook their heads in disbelief at the way gays had been treated.

"I guess we're pretty lucky, huh?" Dakota said, exchanging a look with Cody. They'd both been through a lot in their youth, but they hadn't been hated just for being gay.

"It took a long time, and a lot of protesting to get where we are today," Skyler said. "Shit like Don't Ask, Don't Tell didn't end until Obama."

Jet rolled her eyes, nodding her head. "Oh yeah, that kind of shit was just hateful."

"The trans community is still fighting for rights," Phoenix put in.

"That's right, and that's why we're going to keep fighting," Quinn said, as everyone nodded their heads.

"But we've come a long way," Maggie said.

Everyone agreed with that, and they all started to get up to get on with their night.

"Whatever happened to Danielle?" McKenna asked Maggie as everyone started dropping money on the table to pay their check.

Maggie smiled sadly. "She was found dead in an alley about two years after the riots."

"Oh, Maggie…" Memphis, who was closest to Maggie, moved to hug the woman. "I'm so sorry."

Maggie's tears began as she allowed herself to be comforted by this kind stranger. "They never figured out who did it, not that they really tried."

There were tears from many of the group, as they moved to hug the woman who'd become their hero that night.

"That's not right," Cody said. As a police officer, it irritated her that her fellow officers had treated gays the way they had.

"No, it's not," Quinn agreed, clapping Cody on the shoulder, knowing what Cody was thinking without having to ask. "But you're not like that, neither are any of the cops you serve with."

"They fuckin' better not be!" Jet scowled.

Maggie moved to hug both Cody and Jet with an arm around each of them. "I take it you are officers?"

"In one manner or another," Cody acknowledged.

"Well, you two are the future, now you know what was in the past," Maggie said with kind eyes.

Cody and Jet nodded, accepting Maggie's word on the matter.

The mood of the group that night was definitely affected. They went to Gossip Grill again but didn't really party very much. It was as if they were mourning Maggie's lost love. They talked Maggie into accompanying them to the club and sat with her all night, buying her drinks or anything she wanted. Phoenix even bought her a rose from a passing vendor. It wasn't the night they'd planned, but it felt good to keep company with the older woman.

Later that night, they escorted Maggie home to her apartment in Hillcrest, two blocks from the bar. They made sure she got in, and she kissed each and every one of them in thanks.

Chapter 7

The next morning Remington woke to find Quinn already awake and smoking on the balcony. She saw that she was on the phone, and assumed she was speaking to Xandy. Remi decided to head down to the hotel gym to do her morning workout and give Quinn some privacy.

"That sounds awful!" Xandy exclaimed on her end of the phone.

"Yeah, it was really heartbreaking," Quinn agreed, having just related Maggie's story and how Danielle had been killed two years later.

"What about her friend Christopher?"

"Oh, he made it through the riots, but she said he died of AIDS in the eighties."

"My God…" Xandy breathed. "That makes my heart hurt."

Quinn smiled; Xandy was always very empathetic to other people's pain.

"Yeah, it tore all of us up a bit."

"Did she stay with all of you after dinner?"

"Of course. We made sure she didn't pay for a thing at the club, and we even walked her home to her apartment."

"Aww, that's my White Knight," Xandy said, smiling fondly.

"Bugger that," Quinn growled, blowing out a long stream of smoke. Xandy simply laughed.

"So you're all headed to the parade today?"

"Yeah," Quinn replied, even as her eyes tracked a bird flying toward the ocean. "Feels like it's gonna be hot today though. It's already warm and it's only six here."

"Well, wear sunscreen and don't forget to drink water!"

"Yes, dear," Quinn quipped. "Love you, have a good travel day."

"Send me pictures! You know I'll be bored on the bus!"

"Will do, love."

"Love you! Be safe!" Xandy told her.

"Yes, ma'am," Quinn replied dutifully.

Meanwhile, in another hotel room, Jet was on the phone with her wife, Fadiyah.

"Are you getting a lot of studying done, since I'm not there to be underfoot?" Jet teased.

Fadiyah sighed. "I suppose, but I miss you."

Jet smiled fondly. "Well, you could hop on a plane and fly down here. It's less than an hour…"

At her end, Fadiyah smiled beatifically. Jet had always been a free spirit and a trip to San Diego alone could have brought back that maverick nature. Having her wife arrive could spoil Jet's good time, and yet Jet was inviting her down, actually sounding like she really wanted her there. It did Fadiyah's heart good to hear it.

"I would love to come," Fadiyah swore, "but I have a really important exam on Monday, and I don't feel fully prepared."

Jet beamed, so proud of her wife for her pursuit of a degree, a nursing degree at that. "Well, fine," Jet huffed comically. "Stay there with your books, I will be home before you know it."

"My heart's desire," Fadiyah breathed softly.

"Love you too."

Getting out of bed after they hung up, Jet stretched and walked to the window of her hotel room. Opening the slider, she stepped out onto the small balcony and stared out over the ocean about a half mile beyond. It was a bit overcast, and she could feel the humidity already pressing in. It was going to be a hot, sticky day.

"Bleh!" she commented to no one. Glancing to her right she saw a stream of smoke off the balcony next door. "That you, Sky?"

"No, Devin has taken up smoking..." Skyler drawled as she leaned her head out to look over toward Jet.

"Shaddup!" Jet laughed, craning her neck to see Skyler. "Just didn't know if my eyes were playing tricks on me. I didn't want to wake you two by knocking on the adjoining door and get my privileges revoked by your girl."

"Oui mon ami, wise that," Skyler said, reverting to creole momentarily.

"Is she up?" Jet queried.

"Up and already complaining that the humidity is going to ruin her makeup and hair." Skyler chuckled.

"I'm comin' over," Jet said, leaving the balcony.

"Thanks for the warning," Skyler muttered good-naturedly.

***

At 10 a.m., the Dykes on Bikes led the start of the Pride Parade in Hillcrest. Skyler rode her blue-and-black Harley Dyna Street Bob with Devin dressed head to toe in rainbow garb seated behind her. Jet rode next to them on her silver-and-black Harley. Cody and Dakota rode side by side on their Ninjas. Jazmine, wearing a rainbow bikini with silver heels, rode with Memphis since Dakota's Ninja really didn't have room for a passenger. Dakota had given Memphis a stern look as Jazmine climbed onto the blue Harley Davidson Street 750.

"You take care of my girl!" Dakota warned.

"You know I will!" Memphis told her, running a hand through her white blond spiked hair with the rainbow mini Mohawk.

Memphis, Harley on her blue Harley Low Rider, and Phoenix on her Triumph rode three across.

At one point, the bikes slowed to a stop due to a traffic issue ahead. Phoenix heard someone scream her name over the rumble and whines of the bikes around her. She looked around and saw Michelle, dressed in a sparkling rainbow tutu and a rainbow metallic tank top waving to her. Phoenix laughed, gesturing for Michelle to come to her. Michelle ran over to her smiling brightly.

"You wanna ride with me?" Phoenix asked.

"Wow! Really?" Michelle enthused.

"Sure! Jump on!" Phoenix yelled, even as she gunned the engine, seeing that the group was starting to move again.

Phoenix held her hand out to help Michelle climb onto the bike behind her. "Hold on!" she yelled, as she started rolling again. She instantly felt Michelle's hands grasp at her waist. Glancing back she could see Michelle was laughing as she looked around them. When Phoenix looked over at Memphis, she saw the other woman's eyes lift a couple of times, and she mouthed "Nice."

The parade continued and, as always, the Dykes on Bikes were hailed with cheers and cat calls. As they neared the end of the route in Balboa Park, Phoenix turned her head to look back at Michele, and found that the girl's face was right next to hers.

"Having fun?" Phoenix asked.

"So much fun!" Michelle crowed, leaning in to kiss Phoenix on the cheek. "Thank you for this, it is so great!"

Phoenix inclined her head. "My pleasure."

When they reached the end of the route, the group from West Hollywood rode together to find parking, then got on the Pride shuttle bus to meet up with their friends at the entrance to the festival.

"There they are!" Quinn exclaimed, pointing to the bus as people disembarked.

The group came together and stood in line to get into the festival. The line wound through the grass area outside of the park, with people everywhere fanning themselves. The sun had emerged from the clouds, but the heat and humidity had only increased as the day wore on.

Men and women clad in various outfits of Pride gear did their best to stay cool, as the line seemed to take forever. It was not helped by the fact that a large group of protestors had once again shown up to chant their hate-filled messages.

"Ridiculous," Phoenix growled, as a group chanting something about the "sin" of "Pride" walked by. "Get a fucking life!" she yelled at the group, even as she spied the woman from the night before in the American Flag outfit.

"We have a life," the woman in the American flag shirt and shorts snapped, "a life in God!"

"You go against everything your God claims to stand for," Memphis said, joining the conversation. "Your own Bible says 'judge not, lest you be judged.'"

The woman's mouth worked in frustration at being confronted with facts from her own Bible. "Do not have sexual relations with a man as one does with a woman!" the woman finally spouted.

"Judge not, and you will not be judged; condemn not, and you will not be condemned; forgive, and you will be forgiven," Memphis shot back.

The woman looked visibly shaken at once again having her own god turned against her.

"You're horrible people!" she screeched. "I hope you all die!" With that she moved away from them as quickly as she could which, due to her large size, wasn't very quick.

"Someone should talk to that woman about the sin of gluttony," Michelle muttered, causing the entire group to turn and look at her stunned.

"Holy shit!" Jet crowed and everyone around them burst out laughing.

"Priceless!" Skyler agreed, patting Michelle on the back as she wiped tears of mirth from her eyes.

The group proceeded through the festivals, however, as usual, Remi became the source of major interest, as did Quinn and Memphis. Before long the entire group was feeling overheated and wanted to go somewhere cool for lunch.

"We could hit up The Prado," Phoenix suggested.

"Where's that?" Jet asked.

"It's over there in Balboa Park," Phoenix said, nodding toward the blue dome with gold stars, known as the California Tower.

"Does it have air conditioning?" Kieran asked, fanning herself with a paper fan she'd received from one of the vendors.

"Yes, ma'am," Phoenix replied, winking at her. "More importantly they have margaritas."

"Sold!" Quinn cried.

"Roger that," Skyler seconded.

The group made their way into the park, and to the double wooden doors of the restaurant. There was a half-hour wait, but the ladies indulged in margaritas and ice-cold beers at the bar while they waited.

Once seated, the rather raucous group entertained their servers with their usual witty banter. Starting when the waiter asked to see Memphis' ID for the beer she ordered.

"Yeah, you gotta watch that one," Jet said, winking at Memphis.

"Watch this," Memphis replied, sticking out her tongue.

"Don't stick that out unless you intend to use it," Devin said, pulling a face at Memphis.

"Oh, I'll use it!" Memphis answered.

"Like hell you will!" Skyler protested.

"Take care of your woman, Sky!" Dakota exclaimed.

"I do alright," Skyler said.

"Just alright?" Cody asked, raising an eyebrow.

"You stay out of this," McKenna told her wife.

"Yeah, listen to your woman!" Dakota chided.

Cody reached over and smacked Dakota in the back of the head. "Shut it, Dak!"

"I'll shut something…" Dakota warned as she started to stand.

"You'll behave," Jazmine, who'd pulled on a pair of jean shorts and flip flops after the parade, warned her, a hand on Dakota's arm.

"But—" Dakota protested.

"Uh-uh," Jazmine replied, shaking her head.

The group laughed at the comical pout Dakota pulled.

"Excuse the kids," Remington told the waitress who stood next to her. "We can't take them anywhere these days."

The waitress chuckled. "I've dealt with much worse."

"We're big tippers," Quinn put in from the other side of the waitress.

The waitress laughed. "Better still."

After their orders were taken, the group discussed what they would do after lunch.

"Anyone wanting to go back to the festival?" Quinn asked. "I mean, other than Memphis who has to go back for her set." She nodded toward Memphis apologetically.

Memphis was due to play a set for the crowd for a block of two hours. It was something the committee had begged her to do when they'd heard the famous DJ would be coming down for Pride. In fact, Memphis had been more than happy to accommodate them, thoroughly enjoying stretching her DJ legs again.

"Well, unless Memphis wants us there as moral support…" Harley said, looking to the younger woman.

"Nah," Memphis said, shaking her head. "It's hotter than hell out there, I don't blame any of you for wanting to get out of here."

"We could head back to the hotel and hit the pool or the beach again," Jet suggested.

"Oh, I want to try that ice cream shop down the street from the hotel!" Devin said.

"Oh yeah, me too!" McKenna agreed. "That place looked freaking awesome."

"What ice cream place?" Cody asked, looking mystified.

"They had homemade crêpes and stuff," Devin told her.

"She was busy looking at the Ferrari on the street, remember?" Jet laughed.

Cody had all but fainted when she'd walked by the burgundy Ferrari on the street in La Jolla. While the others had been investigating places to eat, Cody had been drooling on someone's car.

"Oh…" Cody breathed, looking awestruck by the memory. "That 1972 365!" Then she looked over at Jet. "That's a seven-hundred-thousand-dollar car you idiot, you don't see many of those just sitting on the street!"

"Uh-huh." Jet nodded, rolling her eyes.

"Anyway!" Devin put in, before Jet and Cody could get into it over a car. "I want to try that place!"

"Yes, dear," Skyler said, patting Devin on the hand with exaggerated care.

"Don't make me smack the shit out of you, Sky." Devin's smile dripped both honey and venom at the same time.

"Oh!" Jet and Cody said together, causing everyone to laugh again.

"So, sounds like it's ice cream and beach after this?" Quinn surmised, looking over at Remington.

"Anfet," Remington said. "Indeed," she clarified, rolling her eyes dramatically.

After lunch, the group headed back toward the festival area to make sure Memphis got to her DJing gig safely. They were wandering toward the Organ Pavilion and Phoenix was telling them about the various museums in the park.

"The Aerospace Museum is pretty cool," she was saying, when they heard sounded like a scream from far away.

"Did you hear that?" Memphis asked, her hearing used to picking up specific tones.

Everyone stopped, looking toward their left as the scream was repeated.

"Sounds like it's coming from down in the garden!" Phoenix said, pointing to the Japanese Friendship Garden they'd just passed.

The group turned back and walked quickly toward the gardens. Just as they got to the entrance a woman came running out screaming.

"She fell in the pond! She fell in the pond!" the woman screamed.

"Where?" Quinn asked, stopping the woman.

"Down at the bottom of the hill!" The woman pointed frantically.

"Let's go!" Remington said.

The group made their way to the gates, with people pointing down the dirt path that wound its way down to the Koi ponds below. The group began running as more screams and yells could be heard, one of which was, "She's going to drown!"

Quinn and Remington were the first to get to the area where people stood talking excitedly and pointing toward the terraced water ponds and falls. Remington could make out a large woman floating in the water. She immediately headed down into the water, doing her best not to slip on the side of the pond. Quinn waded in after her. The woman was in the middle of the huge expanse of the Koi pond.

"What happened?" Jet asked the people standing nearby, starting to recognize the protestors from the festival earlier.

"She fainted!" one of the younger girls said.

"She was trying to get a better look at the Koi from there," a man in a dark suit said, pointing at the building they were near. "She was bending down, but she must have leaned too far over." He looked sheepish then, not wanting to mention the woman's large size and the possible reason for her miscalculation. "But she fainted, and fell in."

Jet and Skyler exchanged wry looks. "Smart," Skyler muttered.

"We're gonna need you all to move back," Jet told the group.

"Is she conscious?" Quinn asked, as she and Remi reached the woman's motionless form. As they turned her over they realized it was the woman in the American flag outfit.

"Nope," Remi replied. She was tall enough to stand in the pond but could still feel her feet trying to slip on the slick bottom. "Let's get her to the path, then we can start CPR."

Quinn nodded, turning her head to look back at their group. "Someone call 911!" she yelled, then helped Remington lift the woman out of the water.

"Modi!" Remington commented. The woman's limp body was heavier than she'd expected.

"You ain't kidding," Quinn grunted. It took both of them maximum effort to lift the woman and carry her toward the short of the pond.

"Holy shit…" Jet grimaced as she realized exactly who it was that had done a face plant into the Koi pond.

"Fuckin' a…" Phoenix expressed in much the same tone.

"What?" Devin asked. As she was on the phone with 911, she turned around just as Remi and Quinn got to the short. "Oh shit!" she exclaimed. "No, sorry, not you," she had to explain to the 911 operator.

"Lay her down here, on her back," Phoenix said, pointing to a shaded spot on the ground, going into rescue mode. "She probably fainted from the heat," she said, as she moved to the woman and checked for a pulse. "Tell them she's got no pulse!" she told Devin, as she started CPR.

She placed her hands on the appropriate spot on the woman's chest and began compressions.

"You're going to kill her!" one woman shouted, seeing how hard Phoenix was pushing on the woman's chest.

"She's technically already dead," Phoenix snapped, as she moved to give rescue breaths. "If you want her to stay that way, I'll stop," she said, and went back into position to do compressions.

"I'll breathe for you," Jet told Phoenix, kneeling next to the woman's head.

"Thanks," Phoenix said. She was already out of breath with the force she was having to exert to compress through the woman's girth to actually have any effect on her heart.

It was another few minutes until the woman started to cough and gag. Phoenix immediately turned her onto her side so she could spit out the water she'd inhaled. The woman continued to cough and sputter as the sound of sirens could be heard getting closer.

"Someone go direct them down here," Phoenix said.

A woman from the protestor's group and Harley headed up the path to do just that. As they walked Harley turned to the woman and introduced herself.

"Harley Davidson," she said, nodding to the smaller woman.

The woman looked shocked. Harley wasn't sure if it was because of her name or because she'd introduced herself.

"I… I'm Sally," the woman said finally.

Harley nodded at her. As they got to the particularly steep part of the path, Sally's foot slipped and she almost fell forward. Harley reached out, grabbing her hand to keep her from doing just that. Once again, Sally looked surprised by the gesture, but accepted Harley's help to keep her footing.

"Thank you," Sally said softly.

"No problem." Harley smiled.

At the top of the hill they got out to the entrance and could hear the ambulance getting closer.

"It was really nice of your friends to help Jan," Sally told Harley.

Harley shrugged. "It's what we do."

Sally looked back at Harley for a long moment. "What do you mean?"

"Well, Phoenix, the one doing the chest compressions, is a firefighter. Jet, the one doing the breathing, is an agent for the Department of Justice. Quinn is a former military officer in the army and a bodyguard, Remi... well, she's an MMA fighter, but also a bodyguard—they're the ones that carried your friend out of the water."

Sally looked progressively more surprised as Harley named each of the people involved in the rescue. "Wow," was her comment. Then she tilted her head. "What about you? What kind of hero are you?" she asked, her tone a bit awed.

Harley chuckled, shrugging. "I'm just a simple computer genius."

"Is that all?" Sally asked, actually laughing this time.

"Yup," Harley said smiling brightly, just as the ambulance arrived.

Down at the bottom of the path, Phoenix was still trying to assist Jan.

"Ma'am, please just stay on your side, you'll breathe better that way."

"Well..." Jan was saying, looking acutely embarrassed. "I just feel so stupid."

"It's hot out today, ma'am," Remi put in, "could have happened to anyone."

Jan blew her breath out, glancing over at the handsome woman with the dark braids, surprised by the kindness they were showing her. Of course, she recognized the women standing around her and could not believe that they had just saved her life.

"We really thought you were a goner!" Billy, one of the younger boys in the group, told her.

"Yeah, it was really super scary," his sister Jenny, a teenager, said. "Those two got you out of the water!" Jenny pointed at Remi and Quinn.

Jan eyed the two women noting that they both looked very strong, but it was still incredibly embarrassing that they'd had to heft her out of the water. She imagined it had been a real task. She knew full well how heavy she was, and as dead weight she couldn't begin to imagine how hard it had been to carry her.

Jan sighed as her brain desperately tried to reconcile what was happening. They'd already told her that she'd fainted and fallen into the water, and that she wasn't breathing when they'd pulled her out.

Thoughts of what she'd said to this same group earlier in the day echoed around in her head. She'd told them she hoped they died! And it was her that had almost died! And they'd saved her! Why?

"Why did you do it?" Jan asked the woman with the light-colored eyes.

Phoenix looked back at her for a long moment. She recognized the shame and embarrassment in the woman's gaze. Part of her wanted to be nasty, but the part of her that had signed up to be a firefighter to help people won out.

"That's my job, ma'am," Phoenix told her.

"Your job?" Jan queried.

"I'm a firefighter and an EMT."

Jan blinked a couple of times, taken completely off guard by the response.

"I…" she began, unsure how to not only apologize, but thank these women for saving her.

Phoenix's hand on hers stopped her. "I'm glad you're okay."

Jan shook her head in wonder. She couldn't imagine being so kind to her if the roles were reversed. "Thank you," she said, moving her other hand to cover Phoenix's and giving it a gentle squeeze.

Phoenix nodded, accepting the gratitude, even as Jan looked around her.

"Thank you to all of you," Jan said then. "I can't begin to apologize for my comments earlier…"

"No need," Remi said, waving away the woman's apologies. "Viv epi aprann," she said, smiling sincerely. "Live and learn."

Jan blinked a few times, nodding, understanding what Remi meant, and appreciating that they were all letting her off the hook. She wasn't completely sure she deserved to be forgiven so easily, but she also realized that had a lot to do with the character of the people she'd previously cursed.

The EMTs arrived a few moments later, and Jan was put on a backboard. Remi and Quinn offered to help the two young female EMTs carry Jan up the hill, knowing they were daunted by the idea.

"We're old friends," Quinn explained to the EMTs to relieve any awkwardness Jan might feel at the need to have four people carry her up the steep path.

There were tears in Jan's eyes as she was lifted up. It was a moment she would long remember, the moment when she felt God had truly touched her heart and opened her eyes.

By the time they got to the top of the hill, a crowd was already gathering, including a local news crew that had been covering the pride event.

"Bloody hell…" Quinn muttered.

"What?" Remington queried, then she caught sight of the news crew. "Oh, lanfe," saying "oh, hell" in creole.

As they dropped the wheels of the gurney and rolled it toward the waiting ambulance to load her on, the news crew was right there.

"Ma'am, can you tell us what happened?" the newscaster asked, putting a microphone in front of her face.

Quinn and Remi both did their best to ease back out of the cameraman's shot, but Jan pinned them with her statement.

"Those wonderful women, and the two over there," Jan said, gesturing to Phoenix and Jet who'd just emerged from the entrance to the garden, "saved my life!"

The camera swung around to Quinn and Remi as Jet and Phoenix approached. Only when they reached their friends, did Jet and Phoenix notice the camera pointing at them.

"I, uh, oh…" Jet began, putting her hands in the pockets of her black cargo shorts and looking down at her shoes.

Phoenix stood beside Jet, and suddenly found her shoes interesting too.

"And what are your names?" the newswoman asked, as she walked over to the four women.

"That's Remington LaRoché!" the cameraman exclaimed, focusing in on the tall woman. "She's an MMA legend!"

"Ms LaRoché?" the reporter queried. "Would you like to tell us what happened?"

Remi looked anything but thrilled to be the center of attention once again, but she knew she needed to be representative of her friends and allies in the community.

"We simply did what was necessary," Remi said, inclining her head slightly.

"You saved a woman's life!" called someone from the crowd.

"Someone who'd previously called you and your kind disgusting!" yelled a distinctly familiar voice.

Quinn pinned Cody with a narrowed look and the woman grinned unrepentantly.

"Is that true?" the reporter asked Remi.

Remi took a deep breath and blew it out slowly, her lips twitching as she suppressed the urge to cuff Cody upside the head. Finally, she nodded. "Yes, that's true."

The reporter blinked a couple of times, shocked at this new information.

"The lady was protesting at the festival earlier," Quinn commented, doing her best to save Remi from having to comment, knowing her friend didn't like to speak ill of people.

The reporter's look swung between the four of them. "And still you rescued her?"

"A human life is worth more than any retribution," Remi said, sounding surprised that she had to explain that to the reporter.

A smile split the reporter's face. "Not everyone would think that way."

"Everyone isn't Remi," Jet put in proudly.

"And you are?" the reporter asked, immediately charmed by the dark-haired, light green-eyed woman.

"Jet Mathews," Jet replied simply, a crooked smile curling her lips.

"You assisted in the rescue?"

"Remi and Quinn there got the lady out of the water; Phoenix here," she said gesturing to the young firefighter, "did the compressions. I just did the breathing." She said the last with a shrug.

"You performed CPR?" the reporter queried, looking at Phoenix. She sounded shocked, she hadn't realized the extent these women had gone to rescue the woman being loaded into the ambulance.

Phoenix nodded, embarrassed to suddenly have the camera turned on her. "She was in cardiac arrest, we needed to restart her heart."

"Sounding like a true EMT," Dakota muttered under her breath at Cody. Cody nodded, delighted that her heroic friends were receiving some attention for what they'd just done.

"Where did you learn CPR?" the reporter asked, sensing more of a story here.

"I'm an EMT, ma'am," Phoenix replied.

"Wow!" the reporter exclaimed. Then she turned to Jet. "Are you an EMT too?"

Jet huffed out a laugh, shaking her head. "No, ma'am, I'm just an agent."

"Agent? Agent of what?" replied the reporter.

"Of evil…" Cody whispered to Dakota, causing Dakota to snicker, which earned her an elbow to the ribs from her wife.

Jet had the temerity to press her lips together in hesitation, loathe to truly bring her job into the mix. Realizing she didn't have a choice, she thanked her lucky stars she didn't do undercover work anymore.

"I work for the California Department of Justice."

"And you're here for Pride?" the reporter guessed, since Jet was wearing a tank top that said TomBoy X with a rainbow underneath.

"Yes," Jet said, her lips quirked in derision. "Under Midnight Chevalier, you're allowed to be gay and law enforcement at the same time." Her light green eyes widened slightly at the woman as if to say "Got ya!"

The reporter chuckled, nodding her head, realizing how her question had sounded, then she looked at Quinn. "And you are?"

"Wishing I was somewhere else right now…" Quinn answered honestly with a smile, her Irish accent unmistakable. "Quinn Kavanaugh."

"Are you a first responder too?"

"No, ma'am." Quinn shook her head, her bright green eyes dancing with amusement.

"But you are a hero," the reporter said.

"White Knight," Jet put in, causing their group to crack up, and Quinn to turn her head and give her a vile look.

The reporter's openmouthed response meant the term had struck a chord. She smiled as recognition dawned.

"You're the one they call the White Knight!" the reporter exclaimed, looking at the camera. "Quinn Kavanaugh is the bodyguard who came to acclaim during her time as Xandy Blue's bodyguard. Ms. Kavanaugh worked tirelessly to help tornado victims in Kansas, even rescuing Ms. Blue's aunt and two cousins during that same time!" The reporter gestured to Quinn, Remi, Jet and Phoenix. "We have some true heroes among us in San Diego today!"

As the camera turned off, Quinn stepped over to Jet, giving the younger woman a moment of pause as she stared up into infuriated green eyes. To Jet's credit, her intimidation was well hidden under pursed lips of pride.

"What!" Jet exclaimed, raising her arms in protest. "I just said what everyone was thinking!"

"Not the reporter, Mathews," Quinn grated out.

Jet laughed, nodding her head. "I know, I can't believe she didn't recognize you!"

Skyler stepped forward, putting an arm over Jet's shoulder, steering her away from the enraged Irishwoman. "Come on, Jet, I don't want to have to perform CPR on you next!"

Everyone laughed, and the group started toward their original destination, totally unaware that the camera was still recording them.

Chapter 8

By the evening news, the four women were a household name. The reporter had gone to the hospital and spoken with Jan, who'd explained exactly what had happened, and even intimated how she'd treated the group earlier in the day.

"My heart is changed," Jan said, tears shining in her eyes as she spoke to the reporter. "Never in my life have I been shown the way so clearly. The good Lord has made me understand that people are still people, no matter who they love."

The governor, Midnight Chevalier, was even reached for a comment, caught outside of a local restaurant with her husband, Rick Debenshire, and their daughter, Mikeyla. When she was told about what had happened, Midnight smiled, nodding. "I've had occasion to meet Mathews, Quinn, and LaRoché," she said, her eyes twinkling with mischief, "fine women all of them. Apparently, Phoenix Salire is someone to watch for too. These are the caliber of people representative of the LGBTQ community. I'm not sure why anyone is surprised these women helped someone, even though she clearly didn't support their lifestyle. The LGBTQ community is widely regarded as one of the bravest groups of people in society. No matter how much hate and venom is directed their way, they respond with love and pride. Frankly, I'm honored to count many in the LGBTQ community as friends of mine. And I thank and commend these ladies for what they did today."

"Ah hell," Quinn said, as she shut off the news that evening.

The group was back at the hotel after a trip to Scoops, the ice cream shop where everyone, even Remi, had ice cream or freshly made crêpes with ice cream. They'd decided that they all needed to rest before heading back out later that night.

"You knew we were talking to a reporter," Remington pointed out.

"Yeah, but I didn't bloody think they were going to blow it all out of proportion like this!" Quinn blasted.

Remi held up her hand, forestalling Quinn's bluster. "It will blow over."

"The hell you say." Quinn rolled her eyes. "I was just living down that damned White Knight crap."

Remi raised a dark eyebrow. "You don't truly believe that, do you zanmi mwen?" she queried, calling Quinn "my friend."

Quinn blew her breath out in frustration, shaking her head as she picked up her cigarettes and headed out to the balcony to smoke. "Call me stupid!" she called back into the room, hearing Remi chuckle in response.

Sitting down in one of the chairs on the small balcony, she lit a cigarette just as her phone started to ring. Glancing at the screen she saw that Xandy was calling her.

"Aren't you supposed to be on stage in Birmingham right now?" Quinn asked as she answered the phone.

"I'm up next," Xandy said. "Wynter's out there now. So I heard something…"

"Don't start!" Quinn exclaimed. Xandy only laughed at her outburst.

"You really aren't helping yourself here," Xandy chided, even as she smiled on her end. "It's not your fault, you know."

"What?" Quinn asked, brows furrowing at Xandy's comment.

"That you help people and become famous for doing it," Xandy explained.

Quinn guffawed. "Bollocks."

"It's just who you are, babe," Xandy told the Irishwoman. "You're a natural born hero. You might as well get used to it."

"Shut up, you," Quinn told her, even as she started to grin on her end of the line.

Xandy only laughed in response, never intimidated by Quinn's bluster.

"I love you," Xandy told her, "and I love that you have once again proven to the world that we lesbians are good people."

"Don't you do that every night on stage?" Quinn asked. "With every word you sing?"

"Not in a way like you did today," Xandy countered, her voice softening.

"Everyone has their way, love," Quinn insisted. "Today was my way, what you do is yours."

Xandy sighed, loving that Quinn said things the way she did, always supportive, always kind to her.

"You know," Xandy said, smiling brightly, "at this rate, I'm going to have to marry you to keep from losing you to your growing fan base."

"You'll never lose me," Quinn said, narrowing her eyes into the phone, "but if this is your way of saying you want to get married…"

Xandy bit her lip, grimacing, afraid that she'd been too forthright. She didn't risk saying anything else, not wanting to put Quinn on the spot.

"Xan?" Quinn queried when the silence stretched.

Just then there was a knock on Xandy's door telling her she had five minutes before she went on.

"I gotta go," Xandy said, her words tumbling out on top of each other. "I love you! Stay safe!"

"Love you, have a good show," Quinn replied calmly.

They broke the connection, and Quinn sat smoking on the balcony for another half an hour, deep in thought.

That night at Gossip Grill, the group was the talk of the bar. The four who'd executed the rescue were hailed as heroes and were sent drinks all night long. Memphis, who was doing her last night as guest DJ, even resurrected the mix she'd created for Remi's entrance theme from her fight with Akasha Salt a couple of years before. It was an instant hit in the bar and everyone danced.

"So you're headed back to LA tomorrow?" Michelle asked Phoenix. They were sitting outside of the club, after dancing for two or three songs.

Phoenix nodded, taking a drink of the bottle of water in her hand. "Yeah, everyone has to get back to work, and I have to get back to training."

Michelle nodded, looking a bit crestfallen.

"What's wrong?" Phoenix asked.

Michelle shrugged. "I guess I was just enjoying getting to know you again."

"Well, you know, LA is only a couple of hours away, you can come visit," Phoenix said, touching Michelle's hand. "I'll probably be there for another two or three months."

"You wouldn't mind if I came up there?" Michelle's voice held wonder.

"Why would I mind?" Phoenix asked, clearly confused.

Again Michelle shrugged. "I mean, I just didn't…" Her voice trailed off as she realized she had no idea what to say.

Seeing Robin—Phoenix—again had been a wonderful surprise for Michelle. It had been so long since she'd felt a true connection to anyone. Her emotions were a jumble of old connections to her friend, and new infatuation with the woman she'd become. She had no idea what to do with the feelings she was having.

Phoenix watched the emotions play across Michelle's face. Leaning in closer, she kissed the girl softly on the lips, smiling at the shocked reaction she got.

"I would love for you to come up for a visit," Phoenix told her.

Michelle caught her lower lip between her teeth in a shy smile, her expressive brown eyes lighting up at the invitation.

***

Xandy had just finished her latest hit "What You Are to Me," a song she'd written for Quinn, when the lights in FedEx Forum suddenly went down. She looked around at her band, unsure what had happened. Her first concern was the thunderstorms that had been forecasted for the area that evening, but she was sure the show would have been canceled if there was a danger to her or the fans. That knowledge didn't stop her heart from doing minor somersaults in her chest with worry.

Suddenly a single spotlight came on at the side of the stage, and Xandy was stunned to see Quinn walking out. She was further shocked when she realized that Quinn was wearing a sharp-looking black suit with a bright white collared shirt and a rainbow tie. She carried with her a single red rose. Xandy's smile could have lit up the eighteen-thousand-seat forum it was so bright.

"Quinn..." she breathed, elated to see the woman she hadn't seen in months.

Quinn stopped a foot from her and went down to one knee, offering her the red rose, and Xandy was sure she was going to faint dead away. Accepting the rose, even as the crowd went wild, Xandy felt tears sting the back of her eyes. She gasped out loud when Quinn produced a small velvet box from her pocket and opened it, offering it up to Xandy. The ring nestled in rich green velvet was obviously Celtic inspired: a gold interlaced Celtic braid with a large sapphire in the center.

"Oh, Quinn..." Xandy breathed, her microphone picking up every sound.

"Tá mo chroí ina chónaí i tú, tá mo shaol leat." Quinn spoke in Gaelic, her voice picked up in Xandy's mic. "My heart lives in you, my life lies with you," she translated. "Marry me."

Xandy burst into tears, nodding as she bent to kiss Quinn's lips. Quinn folded the younger woman into her arms, holding her close as she cried. The crowd exploded in raucous cheering. At the side of the stage, BJ Sparks stood smiling. Quinn had called him the day before to ask him for a favor. BJ had not only gotten an expedited order from Sheila Fleet from Orkney Island for the ring, but had used his jet to fly Quinn to Tennessee to propose. He couldn't be happier for the couple.

"Technically, I think that's a yes," Quinn whispered to Xandy, who only cried harder as she nodded her head again.

Chapter 9

"You're not nervous, are you?" Jericho asked as Quinn took another curve at breakneck speed.

"Why would I be nervous?" Quinn asked, a dark red eyebrow lifted.

Jericho shrugged. "No reason, you just seem to be a bit… um… rushed?"

"Shut it, Jerich," Quinn growled, as she noted Jericho's amused look.

"It would be perfectly natural for you to be nervous two days before your wedding, you know," Jericho pointed out reasonably.

"I'm not nervous!" Quinn gritted out as she passed another slow-moving vehicle. They were on the two-lane curved Highway 1, headed south.

"Can we get there in one piece?" came the request over the radio.

Quinn glanced up, seeing Skyler's 370Z behind her. Picking up her handheld radio, Quinn keyed the mic. "Yer bitchin' about driving fast?"

"Just about lost a mirror back there," Skyler replied. "I'm sure Devin's freaking out completely in her Hummer behind."

Quinn sighed, she forgot a few of the girls were riding down the highway with them. They were headed from Devin and Skyler's into town.

"Sorry," Quinn radioed, grimacing. She had to admit, at least to herself, that she was nervous, but not for the reasons Jericho probably thought. She glanced at her friend. "I'm not nervous about the marriage, I'm nervous about the wedding."

"Why?" Jericho asked.

Quinn rolled her shoulders. "I'm just worried that things aren't going to go right, and Xandy will be disappointed. This is her 'dream wedding.'" Quinn said, taking her hands off the wheel long enough to do the air quotes to indicate Xandy's own words.

Jericho looked back at Quinn for a long moment, then shook her head slowly. "Quinn, it's her dream wedding because she's marrying you."

Quinn's brows snapped together in surprise at what Jericho had just said. She thought about that statement, obviously it wasn't something that had occurred to her previously.

"But…" Quinn began, her voice trailing off as she shook her head.

"But what? You think it's about the Bel Air mansion? The dress?" Jericho queried disdainfully. "It's about you, my friend."

Quinn's teeth worried her bottom lip, as if she wasn't sure she could believe that. Finally, she took a deep breath, expelling it slowly as she accepted the idea.

The mansion the wedding was being held in belonged to Jordan Tate, who'd happily offered it to Xandy when she'd seen the engagement months before on TV with millions of viewers. There'd been other offers too—BJ Sparks, Cassie Roads, and even Billy Montague had offered up their homes as a place for Xandy and Quinn to be married. Xandy, however, had fallen immediately in love with Jordan and Dylan's home with its enchanting countryside feel, between the lush gardens and winding path shaded by wisteria and jasmine, not to mention the two huge guest houses. Xandy had been completely bowled over. Jordan and Dylan were on tour, so they'd offered the entire estate, which sat on five acres of land in the Bel Air hills. Not counting the guest houses, the house had five bedrooms and a private theater. Most importantly it had a beautiful pavilion surrounded by flowers, where Quinn and Xandy would say their vows, and plenty of room for the reception.

Most of Quinn's large family were flying in that evening for the wedding. Quinn's older sister Fallon had declined to come, which had made Quinn happy. Her sister still didn't approve of Quinn's lifestyle, therefore Quinn didn't want her there. All five brothers, and her two twin sisters, however, were extremely happy to welcome Xandy into their family. Bryan and Brann Kavanaugh had adored Xandy from the first time they'd met her. Four years later, they knew she was good for their daughter, and loved her all the more for it.

Xandy's Aunt Sarah, and her three cousins Bobby, Elly, and Erin were of course going to be present for the wedding as well. Bobby was going to be a ring bearer and Elly would be a flower girl. Neither had ever lost their love for Quinn, always seeing her as their savior after the tornado that had changed their lives four years before.

A little while later, after entering the security code for the gates, Quinn drove up to the Bel Air mansion.

"Bloody Hell..." she breathed, her eyes wide with awe.

"Got that right," Jericho agreed. "You haven't seen the place?"

"Nope, Xandy and Jordan did all the planning here. I was busy guarding Billy, remember?"

"Oh," Jericho answered, rolling her eyes.

Quinn's time with Billy Montague hadn't been without drama—it seemed to cling to Billy like an acrid perfume. There'd been more threats on her life, and a few of DDog's 'soldiers' had attempted to further intimidate Billy. Unfortunately, they'd come up against Quinn Kavanaugh, and found out quickly where she'd gotten her reputation for being dangerous. She'd put three of them in the hospital and had thwarted a final attack by DDog himself at a club opening Billy had attended. DDog was in jail and had been denied bail since he'd attacked Billy on camera. There was no doubt the rapper was done with his attempts to hurt Billy Montague.

As the two got out of the Mustang, Skyler pulled up, followed shortly by Devin's Hummer. They all had the same reaction to the mansion they stood in front of. Just the drive up to the house with its exquisitely manicured shrubs, hedges, and well-appointed patterned, aggregate drive and octagonal courtyard was visually astounding. The house that stood before them was incredible to be sure, with its soaring roof, and elegant stone décor in a beautiful Italian Palazzo style. Even the garage to the right looked like a tiny mansion of its own, with its own decorative aggregate drive.

"And this is how the other half live…" Jericho said, chuckling.

"No kidding," Devin said, "puts my little beach house to shame."

"Don't even think about it," Skyler told her wife. "We're trying to have a baby, not trying to live like rock stars."

"Can't do both?" Zoey asked, winking at Jericho, who only shook her head and chuckled.

"Not funny," Skyler told the younger woman, giving her a pointed look.

Before Zoey had a chance to respond Xandy came out of the house and beckoned them inside.

"Things to do here!" Xandy laughed, as the group hastened in her direction.

Unfortunately, the inside of the house only created more dumbfounded stares and comments.

The dual spiral staircases sweeping down from the second floor, to meet the marble foyer, were only made more spectacular by the multiple windows framed by heavily detailed cornice work. While on the first floor another, much larger, window gave a view of the lush gardens beyond, and above them a vast oval skylight of stained glass depicting the heavens.

"Holy Hell…" Quinn breathed.

Next to her the others simply nodded in mute awe.

"It's beautiful isn't it?" Xandy asked, hugging Quinn's arm as she looked up at the stained glass.

"I would say so," Quinn agreed.

"Wait until you see the gardens!" Xandy enthused.

It was another two hours before Quinn had had the entire tour and needed a drink.

"You'll love this," Xandy said, as she opened the double doors they stood in front of. "Apparently this is Dylan's… ah… 'study.'"

"I've died and gone to heaven," Quinn sighed.

The room's walls were lined with stone, with a hammer beam ceiling looking like a ship hull turned upside down. To the left was a rich redwood, intricately carved bar complete with the back bar and raised shelves, stocked fully with every alcohol imaginable. Around the room were low-slung, comfortable chairs, with a fireplace set in the wall opposite the bar, and a huge TV on the wall above.

"I can see where we're gonna be tonight," Jericho said, grinning.

"Damn right!" Skyler agreed.

"Alright you three," Xandy said, leaning in to kiss Quinn. "Don't get her drunk—her family should be here in about two hours."

BJ Sparks had spared no expense, sending his jet to pick up the Kavanaugh family in Belfast. He'd also hired a limo to bring them all to the Bel Air mansion, not wanting Quinn or Xandy to do much shortly before their wedding.

"I want you to enjoy your time, and your families, not driving back and forth in traffic!" BJ had told them.

Xandy had already set up the two guest houses for some of them, one for Bryan and Brann, Quinn's father and mother, and the other for Quinn's five brothers. Quinn's younger sisters would be staying in the main house with them.

When the doorbell rang, Quinn ran to answer it, throwing open the doors in excitement to see her family. It had been two years since she'd been back to Ireland to see them.

"Well this is a glorious home!" Brann exclaimed, even as she hugged her daughter tightly.

"It's incredible, isn't it?" Quinn agreed.

"It's very grand!" Bryan said in a boisterous tone.

Bryan grabbed his daughter up in a hug.

"How was your flight, Da?" Quinn asked.

"It was grand as well," Bryan said, grabbing Quinn's shoulders and rolling his eyes dramatically. "A private jet! Who would have ever guessed such a magnificent thing?"

"Our every whim was answered," Brann explained, fanning herself as if overcome by the very thought of the grandeur.

"And how did you lot like it?" Quinn asked her five brothers as they descended on her with hugs and chucks on the shoulder.

"There was beer aplenty!" Miles enthused.

"And food, so much food!" Liam said, holding his stomach dramatically. "And not that rubbish they serve on a regular plane! No! It was steaks and lobster!"

"And cakes!" Garran added.

"Even pie!" Hagan put in.

"Then you won't be hungry," Quinn said, grinning widely.

"Posh! We're always hungry!" Miles laughed.

"Don't I know it!" Brann said.

"It was a very nice plane," Finn said, hugging Quinn. "I'm sure Ginny's going to be upset to have missed it."

Quinn nodded. She'd already heard from her mother than Finn and Ginny were separated.

Ida and Margaret, the two twins, moved to hug their sister, after shooing the boys aside.

Everyone greeted Xandy with equal fervor.

"We've got a barbeque going on outside," Quinn told them.

"But let's get you to your rooms first, so we can get you settled," Xandy added.

That night there was a great deal of food and libations enjoyed by all. Xandy's aunt and cousins had driven up, and many of the group were there as well. The celebration of the Kavanaugh's arrival went on late into the night and early morning.

Xandy Blue Hayes woke the morning of her wedding and, rolling to her side, she looked at the woman she was set to marry later that day. Taking in the short red hair, the tattoos, and the strong handsome face of Quinn while she slept, she couldn't help but smile. When she'd met Quinn she hadn't known anything about the bodyguard, other than that BJ had told her Quinn would protect her from whoever was stalking her and sending her disgusting emails.

Quinn Kavanaugh was nothing like anyone she'd ever met before. A tough-looking butch lesbian with an Irish accent. Xandy had immediately assumed that Quinn would be gruff and unyielding; she looked so hard-edged! But right away, Quinn had been a gentle-woman, treating her so carefully, putting her at ease and making her feel instantly safe. What Xandy had felt right off, that had completely surprised her, was a draw to the other woman. She'd never been in anything but straight relationships her whole life, and she'd realized upon meeting and being around Quinn Kavanaugh that she'd never really felt "right" in those previous relationships. Being around Quinn had been so easy, so comforting. It was no wonder she'd started to have deeper feelings for her bodyguard.

The fact that Quinn hadn't wanted to comprise her job as Xandy's bodyguard had been a serious obstacle, and unfortunately had summoned the demons of Xandy's depression. Quinn had been the one to stop her and save her life, changing their relationship forever. Xandy remembered well the feeling of wonder at finally being well and truly loved by someone for who she was, not for what someone else thought she could do for them. It had been a wonderful life since then, and now they were going to be married and truly a committed couple. She still couldn't believe that Quinn had asked her to marry her; she'd never thought that they'd belong to each other in that way. It was something she'd dreamed of doing but had never truly thought that Quinn would consider it.

"What's got you so intense already this morning?" Quinn touched Xandy's cheek, having seen how deep in thought Xandy was when she woke.

Xandy smiled, reveling in Quinn's voice, in her touch, in her bright emerald-green eyes.

"Just thinking about how we got here." Xandy sighed.

Quinn nodded slowly, a smile crinkling the corners of her eyes. "It's been quite a road."

"I can't believe we're actually getting married later today," Xandy admitted.

Quinn canted her head curiously. "Why?"

Xandy shrugged, her blue eyes so vivid and bright in the morning light that Quinn felt a strong tug at her heart. She wanted nothing more than to make this woman happy for the rest of her life. How could she not?

Xandy drew in a deep breath, expelling it with a shake of her head. "I guess I never thought of you as the marrying kind."

Quinn looked considering, her lips pursed. "I guess I never really was," she said, her eyes coming back to stare directly into Xandy's. "Until you."

Xandy gasped at the impact the statement had on her heart; she felt like it was about to burst with joy.

"You always know exactly what to say to make me just want to cry," Xandy told her.

"I don't want you to cry, baby girl," Quinn said, smoothing her thumb over Xandy's cheek. "I just want you to be happy."

"You always make me happy."

"Then I'm doing my job." Quinn winked at her with a devilish grin.

"I think you deserve a promotion, you're doing your job so well."

"I am being promoted, later today. To wife." Quinn laughed.

"Oh, well, alright there you go!" Xandy joined her in her humor.

Later that day as she got dressed for the wedding, Xandy thought back to their conversation that morning.

"Are you nervous?" Devin asked, seeing that Xandy's hand was shaking when she took a sip of the champagne Devin had poured her.

Xandy shook her head, smiling brightly. "No, I'm excited! I'm dying to see how Quinn looks in her tux."

Devin nodded, understanding that feeling fully. She'd been blown away by Skyler's appearance the day they were married.

"Nothing sexier than a butch in a tux," Devin agreed.

"Right?" Zoey added. "I just saw Jericho in hers, and oh my God she's hot!"

"You need to pin her arse down to a wedding date," Kieran told her with a wink.

"Yeah, we've talked about it over and over again, we just can't decide where and how," Zoey said. "Jericho is talking about a 'destination wedding.'"

"Oh that would be fun," Wynter said, as she fluffed her hair in the mirror.

"Give me enough notice, I'll be there," Finley said, even as she continued to work on her hair.

Wynter, as the maid of honor, was dressed in a beautiful sky-blue chiffon dress with delicate ivory flower appliques and a deep V neckline with delicate scalloped edges. The color matched her eyes perfectly. As the bridesmaids, Zoey, Devin, Kieran, and Finley were all dressed in solid sapphire-blue chiffon dresses with ivory flower appliques covering the bodices and necklines that matched Wynter's.

They carefully put on Xandy's dress. It was a vision of ivory and variegated blue orchids printed on silk organza draped over ivory satin. The orchids varied from light blue to midnight blue and adorned the skirt, gathering heavily on the lower two feet of the skirt. The bodice was draped ivory satin. At her throat she wore a necklace given to her by Quinn the night before at their rehearsal dinner: two delicate circles, inside which were two blue enameled swallows in flight. They were beautiful.

"The two of us," Quinn had told her, her eyes shining, "always moving, but never far apart."

From Xandy's ears dangled the matching earrings. They were made by the Scottish jewelry designer Sheila Fleet.

Sheila Fleet's jewelry was something that Quinn loved a great deal. For that reason, Xandy's gift to Quinn had been cufflinks made by Sheila Fleet from the Skyran collection. Quinn already had a ring made by the Orkney designer from that collection. The cufflinks were round with a blue moonstone in the center and blue enamel symbols from Ogham lettering which represented the words "A blessing on the soul."

"And the final touch…" Devin said, as she helped pin on the ivory Irish lace veil that Brann had given to Xandy. "What did you say the story was on this?"

"Quinn's mom gave it to me; it's been handed down for generations in Quinn's family. It's called Carrickmacross lace, and it's been in her family since around early eighteen hundreds."

"Wow…" Wynter's eyes widened. "She must really love you."

"She said that it would have gone to Quinn's sister Fallon as the oldest daughter, but she was too snobby to wear something 'old,' as she put it. So then it would have gone to Quinn next, but…"

"Quinn wouldn't be caught dead in lace anything," Devin put in with a chuckle.

"But Quinn has two sisters, couldn't they have gotten it?" Zoey asked as she admired the length of beautifully made lace.

"I guess so," Xandy said, smiling as she remembered what Brann had told her, "but she said that she believes in her heart that I am Quinn's soul mate, and it was only right that I wear it and pass it on to my daughters."

"Uh, she assumes you and Quinn are having kids?" Kieran quirked an eyebrow at her friend.

Xandy pressed her lips together, her blue eyes shining brightly. "She says she hopes we do, but if we don't, I can hand it down to whomever I feel deserves the honor."

"Are you and Quinn having kids?" Devin had to ask.

Xandy caught her lower lip between her teeth as she shrugged. "It's not something we've talked about, but I'd love to raise a child or children with her."

"Wait, your mom gave Xandy what?" Skyler asked, having just tuned in to a conversation between Jericho and Quinn.

Quinn quirked her lips as she rolled her eyes, knowing this was now going to be a hot topic. "It's just a veil."

"Uh-huh," Skyler muttered, "that's been in your family how long?"

Quinn rubbed her nose in silent agitation. "Just about two hundred years."

Skyler glanced over at Kai, Remi, and Memphis, widening her eyes, even as an evil grin played across her lips. "And what did I hear your mom told her?"

"Shut it, Boché," Quinn growled.

"I think it was that Xandy's supposed to pass it on to her daughter," Memphis supplied helpfully.

Quinn gave Memphis a quelling look. "You…" she uttered in restrained annoyance.

Memphis simply smiled in response, blinking her eyes a couple of time in feigned innocence.

"So are you and Xandy having babies?" Jericho asked.

"I dunno!" Quinn snapped, reaching for the bottle of vintage Jameson's whiskey her father had brought her from home and pouring herself a shot.

"Easy on that stuff," Remi warned, "didn't you say that's like an eighteen-hundred-dollar bottle?"

"Aye." Quinn nodded, her accent very evident suddenly. "And I'm gonna be drinkin' it all myself if you lot don't stop harassin' me."

"Don't be like that," Skyler said, holding up her glass.

Quinn narrowed her eyes at Skyler, but finally gave in, pouring each of them a portion of the amber liquid.

"Have you two talked about kids?" Jericho asked, after they'd toasted and drank again.

"Not really," Quinn responded, "but if she wants them, then that'll be happening."

Quinn looked around at the shocked faces of her friends and shook her head. "My plan is to make her the happiest woman alive," she told them. "If that means kids, then that's what that means."

Jericho nodded, clapping Quinn on the shoulder. Glancing at the clock on the wall in the study they all stood in, she reached for her jacket.

"It's getting to be about that time," Jericho told Quinn.

Quinn nodded, taking a deep breath, and grinned rakishly as she poured another quick drink and downed it. She glanced at herself in the mirror—she had to admit she looked pretty good in the black tux, with the black silk shirt and black tie. Xandy had been more than happy to let her wear all black. She looked around at her friends: Jericho, her 'best woman' wore a black tux, white shirt and sky-blue tie; Skyler, Memphis, Remington, and Kai all wore sapphire-blue ties to match the bridesmaids.

"We look pretty good," Quinn said as they all stood together and looked in the floor-to-ceiling mirror that had been brought in for the occasion.

"Let's go do this," Jericho said.

"Unto the breach," Skyler said.

"Semper Fi," Remi added.

"Oo-rah," Kai put in.

"Balls out!" Memphis exclaimed, to which everyone laughed.

As she stood waiting for Xandy to make her appearance, Quinn glanced around at their surroundings. She and her friends stood in the elegantly appointed courtyard amidst sprays of blue and ivory flowers. Their guests, about two hundred in attendance, were seated under a silk awning, with flowers and vines draped over and around the pillars holding the silk material aloft. As Wynter, and then each bridesmaid made their way down the flower and vine covered pathway, Quinn couldn't help but smile. When Elly, dressed in an ivory satin dress draped with blue orchid flowered organza like the hem of Xandy's dress, and Bobby, looking very handsome in his tux, meandered down the aisle, Quinn felt tears sting the backs of her eyes. It was a beautiful fall day; the sun was shining and the light breeze kept the fresh scent of flowers circulating. Quinn didn't think she could be happier. She was wrong.

When Xandy emerged from the winding path, Bryan, who'd been asked and happily stepped in to give her away, stepped over to escort her down the rest of the aisle, Quinn couldn't believe how beautiful Xandy looked.

"Breathe…" Jericho told Quinn in a whisper.

Quinn chuckled softly because Jericho had been right, she'd forgotten to breathe!

When Xandy and Bryan got to them, Quinn stepped forward, her eyes sweeping over Xandy, tears shining in them. She shook her father's hand, and he leaned in to kiss her on the cheek, then turned to Xandy to do the same.

Quinn stepped over to Xandy, leaning in as she did.

"Tá mé dall," Quinn whispered to her. "I am blinded by your beauty, love."

Xandy bit her lip and smiled. "You look so handsome."

"What's say we get married?" Quinn asked.

"I'd love to," Xandy replied smiling brightly up at Quinn.

"Good thing," BJ, who was officiating the ceremony and had gotten ordained to do just that, told them both with a wink. "Otherwise we're all dressed up for nothin'."

The couple laughed as they turned to BJ, holding hands, and the ceremony began.

A couple of hours later, after the ceremony and pictures, the party really began. Quinn and Xandy circulated, saying hello to their friends and family. As usual the group was hanging out enjoying the festivities. Other big names were in attendance including the members of Sparks, Billy and the Kid, and Fast Lane. Of course, BJ and his wife, Allexxiss, were there, as was the governor, Midnight Chevalier, and her husband, Rick Debenshire. Joe Sinclair and his wife, Randy, and of course John "Mackie" Machiavelli had also been invited.

"Ah, the man that started it all," Quinn said, shaking hands with John.

"If I remember correctly, you didn't want to protect this lovely lady because she was industry..." John joked.

Quinn rubbed the bridge of her nose, looking embarrassed.

"Oh, I see." Xandy laughed.

"As you can tell, I've changed my mind." Quinn winked at her wife and gave Mackie a dirty look.

"Yes, thank goodness!" Xandy agreed.

Phoenix had also come to the wedding, surprised to have been invited. Quinn liked the young firefighter and hoped good things were in store for her. During the rest of her training, Phoenix had hung out with the group and gotten to know many of them much better. Being a general bad ass made her an easy, if temporary, addition to the group of friends.

"Enjoying the party?" Quinn asked Phoenix when she ran into her at the bar.

"This is really awesome!" Phoenix enthused.

"How's Bob? Did you get him released back to the wild?"

"Uhhh…" Phoenix stammered.

"He's okay, isn't he?" Quinn asked, sounding slightly alarmed. Everyone had come to really love the little opossum.

"He's fine," Phoenix assured her. "It's just that I can't release him."

"Why not?"

"He's become too dependent on people." Phoenix shrugged. "It's okay, he can come up to Redding to live with me."

"Good then." Quinn nodded, then her eyes took on a mischievous glint. "I see you brought your friend Michelle."

Phoenix grinned. "She had come for a final visit before I head back up to Redding."

"Uh-huh," Quinn muttered.

"What?" Phoenix queried, noting the odd look on Quinn's face.

"Are you sure that's all? I mean, she's been up here around five times in the last three months."

Phoenix shook her head. "We're just having fun, that's all."

"If you say so," Quinn indicated, patting the younger woman on the back.

"I was happy to see you guys invited Maggie," Phoenix said, changing the subject not too subtlety.

Quinn smiled brightly. "She's my next stop."

"I heard you guys even sent a limo to bring her up to LA," Phoenix went on.

"We didn't want her making the drive by herself," Quinn told her.

Phoenix nodded. "Classy," she said simply.

"Yeah, yeah…" Quinn waved off the compliment, signaling to her new wife to head over to Maggie as she did the same.

Phoenix watched as the couple each walked toward Maggie, who was happily chatting with Midnight Chevalier.

"I just think you are the greatest thing this State has ever had!" Maggie proclaimed, shaking Midnight's hand.

Midnight smiled, looking genuinely pleased by the praise. "That's really nice of you to say, I don't think everyone feels that way though."

"Well, they're idiots!" Maggie rolled her eyes.

Midnight laughed, seeing Quinn coming toward her. "Congratulations!" she said, reaching up to hug the Irishwoman.

"Thank you." Quinn smiled, having liked Midnight more since she'd been determined to get Memphis back from the cult. The woman took no shit, that was for certain. "I see you've met Maggie."

"I have." Midnight smiled over at the older woman.

"Did she tell you about the Stonewall Riots?" Quinn asked, as she held her hand out to Xandy who'd just walked up.

Midnight looked back over at Maggie. "No, but it sounds like a story I'll need to hear."

"It would be my pleasure," Maggie told the governor.

"Maggie," Quinn said, touching the older woman on the shoulder, "may I introduce you to my wife, Xandy."

"This is quite a treat!" Maggie exclaimed, taking Xandy's hands in her own. "You are as beautiful as your voice."

Xandy smiled, biting her lip at the compliment. "Thank you, it's really nice to meet you."

"You've got a good one here," Maggie told Xandy, placing her hand on Quinn's arm as she looked between the two.

"Oh, I know that," Xandy agreed, her eyes shining in the sunlight as she looked up at Quinn.

Maggie smiled sadly but nodded as she did. "This," she said, taking Xandy's and Quinn's hands in hers, her eyes touching on each of them, including Midnight Chevalier. "This is why we rioted. This is why we protested. This is why we made our voices heard."

Xandy's eyes glazed over with tears as she nodded, saddened by Maggie's personal story, but happy at the same time.

"You two were able to marry today, because of what we did," Maggie stated solemnly.

"And we'll always be grateful to you," Quinn said, her tone earnest, "and to everyone that rioted at Stonewall. For all the struggles and the sacrifices, all the pain and misery. For giving us all Pride."

You can find more information about the author and other books in the *WeHo* series here:
www.sherrylhancock.com
www.facebook.com/SherrylDHancock
www.vulpine-press.com/we-ho

Also by Sherryl D. Hancock:
The *MidKnight Blue* series. Dive into the world of Midnight Chevalier and as we follow her transformation from gang leader to cop from the very beginning.
www.vulpine-press.com/midknight-blue-series

The *Wild Irish Silence* series. Escape into the world of BJ Sparks and discover how he went from the small-town boy to the world-famous rock star.
www.vulpine-press.com/wild-irish-silence-series

Lightning Source UK Ltd.
Milton Keynes UK
UKHW011332280720
367302UK00003B/813